KATHLEEN KARR

HYPERION BOOKS FOR CHILDREN

NEW YORK

First Edition

3 5 7 9 10 8 6 4 2

Printed in the United States of America

Library of Congress
Cataloging-in-Publication Data on file.

ISBN 0-7868-1916-2

Visit www.hyperionchildrensbooks.com

Thanks for the Mother's Day present, Suzanne!

CHAPTER 1

Never mind what I'm in for. Where I hang my hat is the Sherborn Women's Prison. That is, I would if I still had one, but they took away my silk straw with its wreath of daisies, like everything else. Along with the rest of my life, I do try to make the best of it.

You can't beat the place for companionship. And mothering. I suppose the mothering comes from my being the youngest inmate in residence. The state of Massachusetts says I'm seventeen, but that's because I'm mature for my age. The truth is I'm sixteen, only there's been a little fiddling with the details for reasons that I won't get into right now.

Mother McCreary is my partner in the laundry room, and she looks after me as good as gold. She's a jolly sort—in for life after having whacked her husband over the head, then chopped him into tiny pieces. She's been beaming ever since. Even the steam and heat of the laundry room never get her down. She just stands there ironing with a vengeance while bellowing vaudeville songs at the top of her lungs. Maybe it's all the steam, but for such a skinny body, her voice comes out rich and deep. I've learned a lot of the numbers from her and naturally join in. So there we were singing away one early spring morning when a stranger waltzed through. And stopped cold, staring at us.

Mother McCreary broke off right in the middle of "Only a Bird in a Gilded Cage." "Well, whatcha starin' at then? Ain't you never seed bloomers done up afore?"

"I certainly have, but never to such accompaniment." Then the stranger smiled—a lovely smile transforming the plain, middle-aged face. "I'm Mrs. Wilkinson, the new chaplain. And the first order of the day, I believe, is to get you two transferred to the garden."

I nearly choked. Garden assignments were the most coveted positions in Sherborn, only given to the most promising. And heaven only knew that Ma McCreary and I were not the most promising. "But—" I began.

"Shut yer gob, Libby." Ma gave me a great poke

with her pointy elbow and squinted at the chaplain through the haze. "What would this be in hopes of, if you please?"

The smile turned on again. "This would be in hopes of saving those glorious voices of yours for better uses." She shuddered. "The best lyric soprano and coloratura I've heard in years, being ruined in all this steam. Now, *that's* a crime." And she spun about and marched out.

"Ma—" I tried again.

"Do-gooders come and do-gooders go, Libby child. The proof of the pudding is in the eating, and we ain't tasted it yet." Launching into "Heaven Will Protect the Working Girl," Ma reached for a fresh hot iron. Throwing all her wiry strength behind it, she set to pounding a nightgown to death.

Sherborn hadn't always been Ma McCreary and vaudeville songs for me. I'd arrived on a cool September day, jammed into one of Boston's Black Marias with half a dozen other women. *Chained* to them. They were drunk. And they weren't very clean. I strove to inconspicuously tug the fine soft wool of my skirt further away from them. My gesture wasn't subtle enough.

"Lookit Miss Prim an' Proper!" the female to my right proclaimed. "We ain't good enough to be near Her Highness!"

"Ain't she headin' for prison, same as us?" The rummy to my left hacked. I thought she was going to spit. Instead, she vomited, barely avoiding my patent coltskin button-top shoes. I jerked my knees together and attempted to protect the entire ensemble with my white kidskin gloves. The creatures to either side yanked on the armchains and roared.

Amidst this jollity the aroma inside the van grew. It didn't improve during the next thirty miles to Sherborn. I squeezed my eyes shut and tried not to breathe. There weren't any windows in the van to see the prison gates, but I knew when we'd arrived. The rear door sprang open.

"Out!" yelled a monstrous woman in a black uniform dress. "You're now in the hands of Bertha Getz"—she smiled a ghastly smile—"chief matron, and your welcoming committee. I'm here to say one thing."

She paused to be certain of our attention. She certainly had mine.

"The downward path and blighted hopes ain't nothing like what you'll see from me if you don't knuckle under and learn the Sherborn rules. *Fast.*"

I shuddered. Bertha. *Big* Bertha. Man-size biceps strained the sleeves of her uniform. Her bun of hair was pulled back so tightly that her thick eyebrows rose in arcs like curling caterpillars. And that mustache—

The chief matron jerked the chains, and I clanged and rattled after the others into some sort of lobby. Here the first rule was explained to us.

"You all heard about cleanliness being next to godliness?" Bertha asked.

A rhetorical question, obviously.

"Here comes your first crack at the Almighty."

Enforced fumigation. I was stripped of my lovely clothes and sent through a torture chamber of foul-smelling tubs and disinfectants.

"But—" I protested, as I was prodded after the harridans to run the gauntlet. "They *need* it, I don't!"

"*Rule Number Two!*" Bertha bellowed. "Never speak unless spoken to by your superiors."

I clamped my mouth shut and came out the other end decontaminated, deloused, and thoroughly humiliated. Next, Bertha and several equally odious henchwomen ordered us to stand at attention. When the bedraggled line—clad only in prison-issue under-shifts—met their satisfaction, another woman made her entrance. I knew instantly this one was different. She lost no time in verifying the fact.

"I am Mrs. Jessie D. Hodder, the superintendent of Sherborn Prison for Women." She stood a safe distance from us, regally poised within stiff folds of gray taffeta. "While you are inmates here you will be under constant supervision. You will learn that *nothing is private*. You will be personally responsible to me for *everything*."

She paused to allow her words to register.

"You are here for a reason—for crimes you have committed. When you leave, your debt to society for those crimes will be paid. Until then, you will be *punished*. I expect you to do suitable penance. I expect you to suffer for your salvation." She glared down the line of misfits. "I expect you to follow our rules."

More rules? There were more.

"All profanity, tobacco, alcohol, and coarse behavior are banned. You will adapt yourselves to a routine of early rising, regular work, and habits of neatness and industry. When you have mastered these, you will become eligible to enter our merit system and receive rewards such as the posting of one letter per month, and the receipt of packages and selected correspondence from the outside world. You may even be allowed the privilege of decorating your own cells. Conform within our system and you will learn that Sherborn's mission is not to raise a *hatchet*, but the *sword* of the spirit against human wrecks such as yourselves."

The superintendent nodded to reemphasize her message and departed, leaving me shivering in my half-nakedness. Also leaving me wondering if Sherborn's merit system was worth attaining. I had no one waiting for a monthly letter. No one anxious to send me packages.

The final insult came next. It was the prison uniform waiting for me: a nasty, scratchy, blue serge dress. To call it a dress did honor to the garment. It hung like a sack. And the shoes they gave me . . . farmer's *boots* were more elegant. Fury fueled my outburst.

"What have you done with my beautiful suit? And my hat?"

"Got us a rebel, have we? Already defying *Rule Number Two*. Straight to your cell without supper," Bertha barked. "It'll be my honor to escort you personally, Your Elegance."

I was shoved down a dark, dank corridor and into a room. It held nothing but an iron bedstead, a washstand, a chamber pot, and a barred window. The door slammed shut. I raced to the tiny open grating set in the door. Defied *Rule Number Two* again.

"When do I get out of here?"

"The most important *rule* of all. When you've figured out you're in prison—and I let you."

Not an auspicious beginning to my new career. I flung myself on the bed and pounded the hard mattress with clenched fists until I'd vented my spleen. A most difficult night followed. When morning arrived, I dragged myself from the bed, washed my face, and straightened the wrinkles in my blue serge.

I'd gotten myself in here. I would learn to play the new game. I'd learn to play by the rules. All but one. From my long night I'd wrested a truth: yesterday's half-naked lineup before the superintendent had been orchestrated for a purpose. It was meant to be degrading. It was meant to emphasize Mrs. Hodder's three critical words about prison: *nothing is private.*

I vowed by all that was holy to keep part of *me* private.

Bolstered by my new resolutions, I was released into my first day of prison life. Unfortunately, my reputation had already preceded me—at least the saga of the journey to Sherborn and my initial reactions to the place. Try living down being a *prima donna*. It was Ma McCreary who saved me. Just tucked me under her scrawny wing and clawed at anyone who gave me a hard time. After a month or two I learned to protect myself. After a month or two, I even began to accept my situation. The uneasy truce lasted until that morning in the laundry. When the do-gooder arrived and Ma's pudding got cooked.

I was filing back to the laundry after lunch when Gladys the trustee pulled me out of line.

"Mrs. Hodder wants to see you immediately, Libby."

The spring went out of my step. Mrs. Hodder's stern gray presence had floated over my days and insinuated itself into my dreams since the moment I'd arrived. The superintendent even put the fear of the Lord into Ma McCreary.

"Gad! Did I overstarch her petticoats? Did I *understarch* them?"

"She was crinkling in fine fettle last I heard."

Gladys tossed her golden locks. She had amazing hair for a woman of almost forty. But then, she'd had the wherewithal to look after it. The girls said she'd made a mint on her "baby farm." That was before the authorities dug up her backyard—and found all the newborns planted in neat rows like cabbages. She'd been looking after the babies for unwed mothers who'd dumped them on her with maintenance money. She wasn't a lifer, but she'd be around a good long time after I cleared out of this place.

Some things I couldn't stomach, and Gladys's scam was one of them. I developed hives just getting too close to her. But she led me up the four flights of stairs and to the superintendent's door before I could even begin to scratch. Gladys wafted away, all affectation. I nearly choked on the woman's conceit—after what she'd done! Then I remembered where I was. And why. I paused to push my steam-limp black hair behind my ears and give a hairpin an extra shove. I knocked.

"Enter."

I poked in my head, then made my body follow.

"Ah, Libby."

"Ma'am." I bobbed a little half-curtsy.

"As you were."

Mrs. Hodder's office was like an eagle's nest sitting in the topmost tower of Sherborn. Her petticoats crinkled as she moved from her desk to the windows overlooking the fortresslike compound and walled grounds beyond. The superintendent focused on the thirty acres of unplowed fields for a moment before abandoning the view to confront me.

"You had the pleasure of meeting our new chaplain this morning while on her exploratory rounds. She comes highly recommended, but does bring some new theories of penology with her . . . such as *reha-bilitation*." The superintendent sniffed. "Punishment isn't sufficient. Mrs. Wilkinson believes in the *reform* of Sherborn's inmates. Even more unlikely, she intends to do this reforming through *music*."

I kept my peace, waiting for the warden to work out the quibbles in her mind. At least I now knew I'd done nothing to get me sent to solitary, like poor Ruby, who lived there nearly permanently. But after all her staring at the fields, I'd probably be reassigned to plodding behind a plow, which wasn't that far up from the laundry no matter how you looked at it.

"Therefore, Libby—"

I snapped to attention. "Ma'am?"

"Therefore, on the recommendation of our new chaplain, I am officially reassigning you to garden duty—your partner, Mrs. McCreary, as well. It's a large concession, as neither of you has yet progressed to that point in our merit system—but Mrs. Wilkinson insists the fresh air is necessary for the health of your voices. You'll begin with potatoes."

"Ma—Mrs. McCreary, too?"

"Yes, but we are concerned with you for the moment." She fixed me with a paralyzing stare. "Prove your worth—if you can. You might be promoted to herbs and flowers. Then again, you might be demoted back to the laundry." Mrs. Hodder crackled to her desk.

I was excused.

"Yes, ma'am. Thank you, Mrs. Hodder." I paused.

"What is it now, Libby?"

"When shall I commence, ma'am? Should I be going back to the laundry now, or—"

"Think it through, Libby Dodge. Do try to develop some common sense. Continue today as usual. Tomorrow you may embark on the garden."

I escaped. Now the superintendent wanted common sense. Wanted me to *think*. She had a point. I'd been avoiding real thought for quite a long time. An empty mind and fine clothing had been my defense against the world—a foolish defense that had left me trapped here in Sherborn.

That night, back in my cell, I gratefully stripped off my huge white apron, then the uniform dress that doubled as a hairshirt. I sat on the edge of my bed in my undershift and drawers, ignoring the chill as I pulled pins to let the heavy weight of my hair fall to my waist. I'd gotten through another day. How many more were there . . . ?

Somewhere beyond the walls of the prison a train whistle blew. Long and low. *In the real world.*

There were too many days. Months and months of them. By the time Sherborn gave me my walking papers at last, 1914 would be nothing but a lost year in my life.

I finally slipped into my flannel nightgown and took the few steps to my windowsill. The geranium I'd babied through the winter had begun to bloom. I inhaled the crimson blossom's bitter scent. The geranium and I understood each other. We were very much alike: both masquerading behind a blithe façade; both vulnerable to the heat and storms of life. Yet our roots were tougher than anyone knew. We would survive.

I touched a velvety petal as the cell lights winked out. Then there was nothing to do but crawl under my blankets and listen to bolts being shot home as the night matron made her way down the long corridor, locking doors. Nothing to do but stare at the cold moonlight working its away across my walls.

CHAPTER 2

There weren't many men around Sherborn, but you can be sure those present were also way beyond caring about the opposite sex. Sparky was a case in point. He was the head gardener, and oversaw the operations on knees that suffered from about eighty years of arthritis. He was a single-minded old coot, too. He gummed a toothless grin at his work crew just after dawn the next morning, rubbed gnarled fingers enthusiastically, and launched right in.

"Tomorrow'll be St. Patrick's Day, me lovelies. You'll be knowing what that means!"

"Whiskey and corned beef!" Ma McCreary crowed.

"Aye, Belle McCreary," Sparky agreed, "but for me, not you. For the likes of you, it signifies that tomorrow is the planting of the spuds."

I glanced up at the sky. The promising sunrise had

quickly faded, leaving in its wake a biting wind and ominous clouds.

"What if it rains tomorrow?" I asked.

"Rain or shine, hot or cold, the potatoes get set in the ground on March seventeenth, St. Patrick's Day. That means today we work the ground and prepare the eyes." Sparky nodded toward the row of hoes sitting in wait. "Get on with it then, dearies."

I grabbed a hoe and sliced through the frost-covered earth. At least I tried to. It was still frozen into hard clods. I turned to Sparky to protest, then realized it was useless. Hot or cold, his potatoes would be planted on St. Patrick's Day. I addressed myself to the task, fulminating against Mrs. Wilkinson. Against do-gooders in general. The heat of the laundry had never called so strongly.

By the time snow began to fall, I was nearly in tears from the cold. My fingers were blue and blistered. I felt giddily feverish. Ma and I had been outside for hours, but the sky did not yet have that noonish sort of light. Well, I could make it with the best of them. I could—

"Miss Dodge! Mrs. McCreary!"

My head jerked up from the hard lumps I was turning. "Mrs. Wilkinson?"

"This is not what I meant by a healthy garden assignment. Set down those tools and return inside with me at once!"

I leaned on the hoe, waiting for the confrontation I knew was coming. The snow was falling heavily now. From the looks of it, we were in for a final wallop from winter.

"Sir!" Wrapped in her cloak, the new chaplain swooped on Sparky. "Why are these women working out here in a blizzard?"

Sparky tipped his cap but remained implacable. "Tomorrow be St. Patrick's Day, ma'am. Potatoes always go in on St. Pat's Day."

Mrs. Wilkinson was already beckoning the other women. "This year the potatoes will have to wait."

The next thing you know, we were all clustered around the heat of the kitchen stoves downing cups of tea. Its steam mingled with that of our wet woolens, filling the room with dissonant odors. Mrs. Wilkinson hovered next to me.

"Did you take enough honey, Libby? Honey soothes the vocal cords."

I tried another sip, then coughed.

She snatched at my cup. "Come along with you. You're spending the afternoon in bed. All I need is you in the infirmary with pneumonia—before I've even had a chance to begin my training program!"

I can't say I'd ever seen my cell at this time of day. I stood dripping just beyond the threshold admiring my geranium surging so spritely between bars toward the frosted panes of glass; the little desk and chair I'd rescued from the basement storeroom and polished; the needlework I'd painfully stitched for my whitewashed wall. Mrs. Wilkinson was admiring my handiwork, too.

"'God helps those who help themselves.' An admirable sentiment, Libby."

"Words to live by, I always thought." Oh, how I'd lived by them; how I'd helped myself right and left. I slumped against the doorpost.

"I like your geranium, too." She set my tea mug on the desk and busied herself. "Let's rid you of these sopping clothes, and get that hair dried. . . . How could they let you work in such weather without gloves, or a hat? It's not humane."

"Nobody ever said we were human, ma'am. Prisoners are just prisoners."

"That remains to be seen."

It was still snowing at breakfast the next morning, and a full foot of the stuff already covered Sparky's potato patch. A blizzard had been brewing, after all. Mrs. Wilkinson took full advantage of it. In the middle of our porridge she arrived like the lost spring, pert in a lavender-striped frock with dainty collar and cuffs of white organdy. Her shining brown hair was neatly done up in a loose bun that settled on the back of her neck—and the prettiest little pearl studs decorated her ears. I was close enough to note that they were real pearls, too. Something I knew a thing or two about. My fellow inmates were drinking in this vision as greedily as I. We were all fashion-starved. Then she cleared her throat.

"Good morning, ladies. I'm here to ask for volunteers to begin a prison choir." She smiled brightly and waited. Silence was the only response from two hundred faces. Mrs. Wilkinson took a deep breath and tried again.

"Perhaps I should make myself clearer." She upped

her volume. "Due to the inclement weather, Mrs. Hodder has given me permission to hold choir auditions this morning. All volunteers will be excused from their ordinary work—"

Well, then she nearly had a riot on her hands. Everyone volunteered. Mrs. Wilkinson found it necessary to arrange her "auditions" by work department: first the outside crews, who were snowed in anyway. After them would come the laundry women, then the sewing-machine shop, and finally the kitchen staff. Ma McCreary and I got to the head of the line for the garden crew, but it wasn't necessary.

"You two have already auditioned." The chaplain pulled us out of formation. "I'm promoting you to assistants. Keep the volunteers organized and quiet and march them to the assembly room."

Ma grinned. "You all heard what the lady said. Fall in place and don't stop till you hits the pianner. Ready? *Hup! Hup! Hup!*"

What a to-do followed! Mrs. Wilkinson could play the piano fine, but it was so out of tune that she finally had to give up on it and work with her pitch pipe. That, she explained, was the little whistle-like thing she blew into that always gave the right note.

"Well, I never!" Ma exclaimed, pressing so close in admiration that she nearly shoved it down the chaplain's throat. "That there little gadget does just the same thing as my throat!"

"Not all of us have perfect pitch," Mrs. Wilkinson drily commented. "If you'd just give me a little breathing room, Mrs. McCreary?"

Ma backed down and Mrs. Wilkinson moved on to her first test. It was *a cappella*, as she called it, meaning singing without musical instruments.

Such a warbling and caterwauling! Before the hour was out I wished I had a wad of cotton to stuff in my ears. We were treated to several renditions of "Onward, Christian Soldiers," and too many of "Rock of Ages," until Mrs. Wilkinson held up a hand to halt the proceedings.

"Anything but more threadbare hymns, ladies. Please. Our choir will be *different*. Easter is coming. The Resurrection! If I can only find enough voices I mean to see it in with a greater glory than you have ever heard!"

She paused to see if she had our attention. She did, sort of. Except for Ruby, who'd just been let out of solitary and was cross-legged on the floor, stringy hair falling in matted strands to her waist, beating out a song that only she could hear. Mrs. Wilkinson stepped over to her, stooped to gently catch her hands, and looked into her eyes.

"My dear—"

"That'd be Ruby, Boss," Ma helpfully explained. "She ain't always with us."

Second-Story Sal snickered. "How could she be? Ruby's always in solitary detention!"

"Why?" Mrs. Wilkinson raised her head.

"'Cause she's feebleminded, can't you tell?" Kid-Glove Rosie added.

"No, I can't tell. Stand up for me, Ruby."

Ruby rose, still humming to herself.

"Now sing the song that's in your head, Ruby."

"Out loud?" she whispered.

"Please, dear."

Ruby launched into "Home, Sweet Home." She sang it all the way through, adding verses I'd never heard. She started out really tentative, but by the end her voice was pure and clear, and there wasn't a dry eye in the room.

Mrs. Wilkinson fumbled for a handkerchief and blew her nose. "Congratulations, Ruby. You now belong to the choir."

"Me?" Ruby flopped onto the floor again and rocked with pleasure.

Mrs. Wilkinson shoved the handkerchief into her sleeve cuff. "Obviously a discussion with Mrs. Hodder on the evils of solitary confinement is in order. . . . But getting back to business in the here and now, it's Handel I mean to do. His 'Hallelujah Chorus' set for female voices. It's usually performed at Christmas, but we'll be taking enough other liberties that I hardly think it matters during which season it's sung. By Easter you will know who Handel is. And you will understand his music. Next!"

It took all day and all the way beyond to lights out, but by then every inmate in Sherborn had been tested. Mrs. Wilkinson had her choir—fifty-five voices strong.

As the snow slowly melted, Sherborn began moving to a different tempo. Mrs. Wilkinson convinced the superintendent to shorten work periods so that she could fit in a choir practice each afternoon. Funny how with choir to look forward to, the same amount of work got done in less time. When afternoon sessions weren't enough, Mrs. Wilkinson squeezed in another hour before lights out. She managed this by simply having lights turned out at ten, rather than nine. This took a little more convincing with the powers that be. It was a discussion the entire choir was privileged to overhear when Mrs. Hodder stopped by to listen in on the end of one of our first afternoon practices. I watched her wince. As the chaplain abruptly lowered her conducting arm to silence us, Mrs. Hodder spoke.

"Do I detect a certain dissonance among some of the voices?"

"Of course you do," Mrs. Wilkinson tartly replied. "I barely get them warmed up when it's necessary to stop for supper. The quality is there—I just need more time to bring it forth."

"I'm running a prison, Mrs. Wilkinson, not a music academy. Rules, regulations, and schedules are of paramount importance. And you've already disrupted my schedules—"

"But positively, Superintendent. *Positively.* Surely you've noted the change in atmosphere—"

"The governor and Prison Board never requested happy inmates, Mrs. Wilkinson. They are here for *discipline.* They are here to atone for their misbegotten deeds."

"Perhaps a little happiness might make them rethink repeating those deeds when they return to life outside these walls. Singing makes all of us happy, Mrs. Hodder. And I need more time to focus on the *quality* of this singing before Easter. With a little more concentrated effort, I strongly believe that the new Sherborn Women's Choir will be impressive enough for you to invite the governor and the board to our Easter service."

Mrs. Hodder blinked and crinkled her skirts. "The governor? The Prison Board?"

"A nice little feather in your cap," Mrs. Wilkinson suggested. "And I wouldn't be expecting any more work time—"

Mrs. Hodder reached for the chaplain's arm. "Let's finish this discussion in the privacy of my office, Mrs. Wilkinson."

Mrs. Wilkinson nodded at us. "Choir practice is over for this afternoon. You may go along to your suppers, ladies."

The late practice became official, and to the delight of one and all, every inmate was invited to attend. Once again, the superintendent had her doubts about allowing so much liberty to her charges, but Mrs. Wilkinson sweetly overcame them all. She had only one rule: no chatter from the audience.

It was an unexpected entertainment, even for those who didn't have the voices. The listeners brought along their knitting and crocheting, and the click of all those needles added a constant touch of percussion to the newly tuned piano. Slowly we learned who Handel was.

"A truly great German composer, ladies," Mrs. Wilkinson began explaining.

"He still with us?" Ma wanted to know.

"Unfortunately not. He died over one hundred and fifty years ago—"

"Pooh!" Ma exclaimed. "He weren't in vaudeville, then."

"Hardly. But in his mind's eye George Frideric Handel had a better audience—"

"Ain't no better audience than them what hangs around the Boston Colonial. Only thing I regret about doin' the dirty to my Harold, that's missing them shows on Washington Street, a mug of beer in my hand. Singin' along—"

"Mrs. McCreary. If you please."

"Sorry, Boss."

The chaplain began again. "Handel composed his *Messiah*—from which we are borrowing his 'Hallelujah Chorus'—under the influence of great emotion. He said, 'I did think I did see all Heaven before me—and the great God himself!'"

Ruby, huddled on the floor in the front row, gave a huge sigh. Mrs. Wilkinson paused to pat her head. "I do believe you will see the great God in his music, too, Ruby. But first we must prepare our voices. We must learn to mellow them, to soften the harsh edges acquired through improper usage."

All the chaplain's fancy language came down to one thing: scales. We learned to sing scales up, down, and in every direction known to man—or at least to Mrs. Wilkinson.

All the while, the real spring gradually arrived.

"Hey!"

I was the first one to notice.

"Sparky! Ma! Everyone! Our potatoes are coming up!"

Sparky hobbled over to my row to admire the tiny, tender, emerald-green shoots just beginning to peek above the ground. He painfully bent to croon to the nearest. "Aye, there you be, my beauty. Coming to show off to the sun. Such fine spuds you'll be making!"

Sparky's ecstasies over his plants did not normally move me. Today I knelt right beside him and did a little crooning of my own. Here was something new and real that I'd helped to create. I'd never done that before. Not even my geranium had started from scratch—just as a clipping from one of Ma's plants. Sparky and I shared a grin.

"Ain't God's earth wonderful!" he said.

"Yes." It was, too. I'd never known that before. How could I have? I'd never stepped foot in the country before Sherborn, and I'd arrived here in the dark confines of the Black Maria. The closest I'd ever come to greenery was promenading on the Boston Common, and the occasional summer excursion to Wonderland—the amusement park just outside the city—as a reward for jobs well done.

I turned to Sparky. "What do we plant next?"

CHAPTER 3

There were no more lovely frocks to drool over. Mrs. Wilkinson wore sensible working skirts and shirt-waists for the tough practices as Easter closed in on us. But her costume was always complemented by those little pearl studs. It took a while, but I finally found out why. And it was Gladys the trustee who let it slip.

Gladys worked as a secretary for Mrs. Hodder, so had access to office gossip and even some of the files. She offered her classified information only on a barter system: a rare portion of dessert; a length of lace for her undergarments; shared shampoo from home packages to keep her fine hair glistening. Gladys had been a businesswoman for too long not to know when there was an advantage to be had. Our pasts were meant to be a closed book. No one was supposed to know *why* we were in Sherborn unless we chose to offer it ourselves. But Gladys dealt in curiosity.

Ma McCreary never hid her deed. Why should she? She was pleased as punch to have found a solution to a husband who regularly beat her to a pulp—and a church that wouldn't allow her to divorce him. Second-Story Sal was also free with advice on how she'd pulled her famous burglaries. "Not many women in my field," she'd brag, her enthusiasm lighting up her narrow face under its halo of brown frizz. "I was right up there with the best of the men!"

Others among the women were equally forthcoming. Molly Matches claimed to be the most efficient of arsonists for hire. "You want a building razed fast and clean, it takes a woman's touch. No man can do neat and tidy like a woman. It's a science, it is. And not a single accidental death on my shoulders." She nodded her fire-red head for emphasis. "I pride myself on that."

The chastity offenders, like Flo or Emma or Rachel, were less anxious to broadcast their histories as streetwalkers. Only Verity—not much older than I, but tough as nails—admitted that it was a "sheer pleasure" to have a year's break from her profession.

"What—you'd return to it?" I asked her.

"I'm not educated like you, Libby," she answered.

"What else can I do? Starve on wages from twelve-hour days in a factory? That's for mugs. Prostitution pays better. It's a business, like any other."

I shuddered at the thought. It certainly didn't seem like any other business to me. But she *was* right about the education part. I had been blessed with a little learning, even if it was not quite the conventional sort. . . .

But getting back to Gladys, I finally succumbed to curiosity over Mrs. Wilkinson. Odious though it was, there were negotiations. The promise of five future desserts (Gladys did have a sweet tooth) gave me the information that our chaplain's late husband had been a baritone with the D'Oyly Carte Opera Company, and she its chorus mistress. Not worth five desserts, but it did explain the music. The last tidbit was worth the sacrifice, though. It explained the earrings, too. For Mrs. Wilkinson's first name was Perle.

Somehow the name pleased me. I puttered around the garden for a few days planting kohlrabi and turnips, chanting "Perle, Perle, Perle." A pearl wasn't all cold glitter like a diamond. It didn't have the loud, rakish brilliance of a ruby or an emerald. A pearl was built of layers, gaining strength and luminescence with each new one. A pearl grew from life. Maybe someday I could grow—like a pearl—into Mrs. Wilkinson's quiet beauty of spirit.

Easter was almost upon us, and we'd graduated from scales to Handel himself. There really weren't all that many words to graduate to, though, and those few— as Mrs. Wilkinson explained—were taken from the book of Revelation. I'd had more preaching done to me at Sherborn than during all the rest of my life combined. I'd learned a few things about the scriptures— yet I can't say that Revelation would have been my first choice for comfort. But these words had a power and magnificence I'd never known. Set to music that I could sing, they began to make me feel as though there might be power growing within me, too.

All through Holy Week Ma and I went about our garden work bellowing: "Hallelujah: for the Lord God omnipotent reigneth!" As Good Friday approached we moved on to:

The kingdom of this world is become the kingdom of our Lord, and of His Christ; and He shall reign for ever and ever. King of Kings, and Lord of Lords.

Then Easter Sunday arrived. *Hallelujah!*

Superintendent Hodder had been seen quietly slipping into the rear of the assembly room on more than one of our final rehearsals. Apparently what she heard emboldened her. She swallowed hard, took the chance, and invited a few worthies to attend the planned sunrise ceremony. Mrs. Wilkinson insisted Easter Sunday would be fair, and decreed that the piano be hauled to the courtyard the day before. Ma and I oversaw the exertions of Sparky and a few of the sturdier inmates, one eye always directed at the sky with apprehension.

"Do take a care, Sparky," I begged. "We don't want it to be jostled and go out of tune."

"Then Sherborn should've brought in some young bucks for the job," Sparky groused. "Me shoulders ain't what they was—and me knees—"

"Sal! Verity!" Ma barked. "Take the front weight! His knees are crumbling!"

I held my breath as the instrument slowly tottered across the courtyard to the final position chosen by the chaplain. It was in the shadow of the dormitory block behind it, surrounded on either side by wings bristling with turrets, towers, and chimneys. The formidable buildings cut off all views but the one the choir would face: the view to the east, open and clear to the gate and fields beyond.

"Now! Let it down right there!" I ordered.

The piano settled onto the gravel with the slightest sigh of strings. I trotted over, tarpaulins in hand. "Thank you all so much!"

Verity reached for the heavy canvas. "I can protect it for you, Libby. You worry about the sunrise."

I did worry, making that night my second longest in Sherborn. It was for a different reason than the September evening of my arrival, though. I kept crawling from bed and staggering to the window to check the weather. No, there wasn't any frost to harm the piano. Yes, there was still a moon . . . now it was descending, and the stars grown brighter . . . till even the stars began winking out. There would be a sunrise for Easter morn.

Fifty-five strong, the choir of Sherborn took its place on the wobbly risers Sparky had cobbled together for us behind the piano. The chairs in the front of the courtyard slowly filled. Mrs. Hodder hadn't managed to entice the governor himself, but there was a select group of wealthy do-gooders, social workers, and city officials from Boston—all come to see what could be done with their "incorrigibles." Behind these chairs stood the rest of Sherborn's inmates, freshly bathed and primped and shivering in the dawn chill. When stripes of pink began stretching above distant hills, Mrs. Wilkinson swept into the courtyard, splendid in an Easter ensemble of daffodil yellow. She paused before the piano, blessed every single one of us with her smile, then turned to our audience.

"Welcome. Welcome to this celebration of the Resurrection of our Lord—and the resurrection of our Sherborn women."

The sun began creeping over the eastern horizon, and Mrs. Wilkinson spun to her piano. With one more special smile directed to us—her anxious choir—she began to play. My throat felt too dry to utter anything but a croak, yet when the chaplain lifted a hand to begin conducting, the voice came. The words came. The music came. As the sun grew into a shining ball we sang with our hearts and our souls.

"Hallelujah! for the Lord God omnipotent reigneth!"

Our voices blended, high and low. Our hidden power flew into the morning, over the heads of the important people, past our fellow inmates, through the sky and into the very heavens above. I could feel it. It was happening.

We sang the final chords with the sun beaming upon us. A long moment of awed silence followed. Then came the applause. It continued while Mrs. Wilkinson rose from her piano to bow first to the audience and next to us. Tears were streaming down her face. She didn't even bother to reach for her handkerchief.

"Thank you." Her face radiated more light than the sun. "Handel would be proud."

There were hot-cross buns for breakfast, still warm from the oven. As many as we could eat. Ma sat next to me, gorging. I nibbled at the edges of a bun, tentatively tasted the sweetness of the icing, then set the whole thing down on my plate.

"Where'd that long face come from, Libby?" Ma asked as she stretched over me for another treat from the heaping platter before us. "We did a bang-up job, didn't we?"

"Yes, but . . ." I had the strangest urge to cry. Not just cry, but bawl like a baby. Bawl like I hadn't for years, not even when I'd been pinched by the police and knew something was over for me. It had been a kind of relief, that arrest. . . . I swiped at my eyes.

"Here." Ma shoved her handkerchief at me. "It'd be the letdown, is all. Jest like after birthing a child."

I sniveled past the lacy edges of her square of fine linen. Such a strange thing for Ma McCreary to own, so delicate. I swallowed a sob, then gave in. "What's to come next, Ma?" I cried. "What could possibly be as beautiful as what we just accomplished? What's to happen to our choir now that our concert is finished? I don't think I can go back to the way it was before!"

Mrs. Wilkinson suddenly appeared behind me. "Libby. Handel was only the beginning."

I swiped at my eyes and managed to look up. "Only the beginning?"

"Of course. We'll be moving on to something else. Not as glorious in the same way, but just as grand."

"Are you certain? Can you promise? Would the superintendent really allow—"

At that very moment Mrs. Hodder herself bustled into the dining hall, followed by her group of worthies. She paused importantly to gesture toward the assembled.

"And here you have our choir—and our other inmates—enjoying a special treat for Easter breakfast. Discipline isn't everything, ladies and gentlemen. *Atmosphere* has a great deal to do with renewing these lost souls. Positive training in the finer pursuits of life, such as music, can make all the difference in rehabilitation. A *happy* inmate is much more likely to return to the world as a new and invigorated member of society."

My mouth dropped open. This from Mrs. Hodder? Had the Easter spirit resurrected something in her as well?

"Will there be more performances, then, Superintendent Hodder?" one of the gentlemen inquired.

"More performances? Oh, yes. Indeed there will be!"

"Please remember to keep me on your guest list," chirped an expensively dressed woman. "I do believe this was the finest Handel I've ever been privileged to hear. So dramatic. So heartfelt."

"But of course, Mrs. Simons." Mrs. Hodder waved her guests forward pretentiously. "Now I'll just show off a few of our cells before you leave. Mrs. McCreary, our lifetime guest, has crocheted the neatest little doilies to decorate her rocking chair—"

As the very important people disappeared, I glanced at Ma, whose jaw had dropped open wider than mine at the mention of her name. While she tried to close it, Mrs. Wilkinson sank into the empty chair next to me as if her knees had just given out the way Sparky's did. "I believe I can keep that promise, Libby. And I think I'd like one of those hot-cross buns myself."

CHAPTER 4

Easter Monday it was back to work assignments as usual. Ma still hadn't gotten over being singled out to the Boston worthies for her crocheting skills. As we worked our way down long rows pulling weeds, she nattered about it.

"Doilies is all fine and good, but there's only so many doilies can be scattered about a room what's six foot wide by ten foot long. Seems to me as a 'lifetime guest' I ought to be given a few more feet."

"But the bigger cells are only for the honor class, Ma," I reminded her.

"*Humph.* Honor class. Never find me sweetenin' up to Big Bertha and Mrs. Hodder like Gladys. Ought to be a different kind of merit system. The kind what takes into consideration someone who's had the strength of character to rid the world of Harold McCreary. There wasn't never an ant nor spider he wouldn't go out of his way to crush. When he weren't

torturing me or poor innocent children and animals."
Ma considered. "Come to think on it, it were only
cockroaches and rats he let be. Must've considered
'em relatives. Like I says, it were a service I performed."

I eased my back to try to get rid of its stitch. "I'm
not sure the authorities look at it that way. If they
considered these things from a political or humani-
tarian point of view, I might be in the clear, too. I
could call myself a socialist, and claim what I'd done
was part of saving the world from the excesses of cap-
italism—"

Ma's eyes darted up from the ground. "And what
was it you actually done, Libby?"

I tossed aside a handful of weeds and hunkered
down over my row again. "Oh, it doesn't matter.
They're throwing Wobblies in jail, too."

"Them International Workers of the World? The
same as goes around the country tryin' to upset and
unionize hardworking laboring men? Don't never tell
me you was an *anarchist*, child. At your age?"

"In a way, Ma. In a way." I moved down a few yards
to a fresh patch of weeds. It was becoming harder
and harder to keep that little piece of myself private.

Especially from Ma McCreary. "We've got choir practice again this afternoon. What do you suppose Mrs. Wilkinson has up her sleeve for our next performance?"

Ma shrugged in defeat. "Hope your secrets keeps you warm at night." She attacked a weed as if eradicating a terrorist. "Who knows about the choir? But gettin' back to my room—"

"Your cell."

"*You've* got a cell. *You'll* be leaving. A body of my status longevity-wise can call it a *room.*"

I couldn't help it. That started me giggling. Then we were both laughing, and then it was time for lunch.

I guess I was still a little giddy from yesterday's success. The other choir members were, too. When Ma and I got in from the garden, we found a bunch of them strutting around the dining hall rearranging the usual orderly rows so we could all sit together. Sal and Rosie were shoving two of the long trestle tables together. Flo was snatching chairs right and left.

"Ma, Libby!" Molly Matches yelled. "Saving places for you right here with the rest of the choir!"

"Shoulda thunk of it sooner." Ma swaggered off past tables full of non–choir members suddenly turned sullen. I sashayed right behind. There was some mumbling as we walked past, but I ignored it. The Sherborn Choir *could* do something these other women couldn't do. So maybe we did show off a little. I still didn't expect what happened next, after the food arrived.

Agnes started it. She was sitting at a non–choir table next to ours. Out of the corner of my eye I noticed her reach for one of those rock-hard little rolls the kitchen kept producing. She brought it to her mouth as if to take a bite, then stopped to study it. Next she was winding up her arm like a stickball pitcher on one of Boston's street teams. She let fly.

"Damnation!" Second-Story Sal caught it in the eye—and flung it back.

That was all it took. Soon rolls were flying fast and free all over the room. The buttered ones were the nastiest. Ma got one caught in her hair when she didn't duck fast enough and joined in the fray with gusto. Someone thought to add a tough little nugget of meat from her stew to the mix, then bowls followed, gravy and all.

I was tempted. I'll admit it. I even had the last remaining roll from our table in my fist—when Verity leaned over and knocked it from my grasp.

"What—"

She nodded toward the door. A phalanx of guards had appeared from nowhere. The matrons had had an easy life here at Sherborn lately. Ever since the music began, they'd minded their business if we minded ours. But we'd crossed the line. Broken the rules. Revenge was swift.

It was an unsettling sight watching a dozen hefty, stern-faced women—hair pulled into painfully severe buns in emulation of their leader—march into the center of the room. Flying missiles crashed to the floor. The sounds of crockery shattering like bursting bombs died in a great vacuum of silence.

"Who started this?" roared Big Bertha. She was still the toughest of the guards. Still in charge. As if to prove it, her mustache bristled.

More silence. But a few eyes drifted toward Agnes. It was enough. Bertha yanked her from her chair.

"It's solitary for you!"

Agnes didn't go quietly.

"What about Sal? She threw my roll back!"

Sal lunged from our table toward Agnes. "Ain't nothing worse than a *snitch!* I'll fix your bonnet good an' proper, Agnes Cordoni! Just let me get my paws on you—"

She did. For a moment. Fists and hair flew gloriously.

Then Sal was invited to join Agnes. Then the rest of us got locked into our cells for the afternoon.

Choir practice was canceled indefinitely.

A full week passed—a full week without music in our lives, without music in my life—before our punishment was deemed sufficient. It was a wan, meek, and penitent group that finally faced Mrs. Wilkinson. It was also a group monitored for the very first time by Big Bertha. Mrs. Hodder wasn't taking any chances. The matron spread her legs beneath the long skirt of her death-black uniform and folded her beefy arms, settling her two hundred-odd pounds right next to the piano like a boulder. Our chaplain looked at her. I thought I caught her shivering delicately.

"I believe the rear of the room will be a sufficiently secure position, Matron Getz."

Big Bertha grunted, but she moved. We all turned toward the piano again, sprawled ourselves across the wooden planks of the floor, and forgot about the heinous creature.

"Well," was how Mrs. Wilkinson finally began when she took over control of the assembly room. "Well."

"They started the fight," Ma protested. "Not us!"

"But you chose to continue it, Mrs. McCreary."

Ma dropped her chin clear down to her scrawny chest.

Mrs. Wilkinson sighed. "Enough. We'll begin anew. In the intervening days I've had more than sufficient time to analyze the situation. Envy is what we are dealing with, ladies. *Envy*. One of the Seven Deadly Sins. Not to mention *Pride*. Another one of those sins. We could throw in *Wrath*, or anger, quite easily as well. None have a place in your lives here at Sherborn, or in your lives *anywhere*."

We were all sort of hanging our heads by this time.

"It's just not Christian"—she continued—"to have any of these feelings. They're totally uncalled for and unnecessary. God blessed you all with lovely voices. What is necessary now is to determine what these other women have been blessed with. . . . And to give them their own chance to shine." She stopped. Waited.

"All right, then." Ma spoke up first. "That Agnes— well, she can sew up a storm on them Singer machines they got in the sewing room. Used to be a dressmaker afore the drink took her."

"Aha!" from Mrs. Wilkinson.

"Freda and Fanny Snodgrass—the Swindling Twins? They're pretty good, too," Second-Story Sal admitted. "And Mildred—Mildred claims she was in millinery."

Mrs. Wilkinson's eyes took on their old sparkle. "Excellent! There couldn't be better news!"

"How you figure that?" Ma asked.

"A full team is what we need for our next production, ladies. If we make these women part of our team, not only will they not feel ignored, but we can produce the most spectacular show ever to be performed on the boards of Sherborn—or anywhere else!"

By this time I wasn't caring about teamwork. I was well and truly overcome with curiosity—for all I knew another one of those Deadly Sins. But there was no squashing it. "What in the world is this show?" I asked. "What are you planning for us, Mrs. Wilkinson?"

She stretched her five-foot frame proudly. "What I am planning is to produce a full and complete production of Gilbert and Sullivan's *Pirates of Penzance!*"

Mrs. Wilkinson's eyes darted around, looking for a match to her excitement. What she got was more silence, just as heavy as after the food fight. It was Ruby who finally broke it.

"Please, ma'am?"

We couldn't usually hear Ruby's whisper, but this time it filled the room.

"Please, ma'am. What is that?"

Mrs. Wilkinson's shoulders slumped. I watched her make a mighty effort to raise them again. "*Who* and *what*. The *who* are W. S. Gilbert and Sir Arthur Sullivan. The geniuses who took the civilized world by storm with their comic light operas in the last century. The *what* are the operas themselves: *H.M.S. Pinafore. The Gondoliers. The Mikado.* You must know them!" She turned to Ma. "Mrs. McCreary. Surely in your vaudeville days you've heard of the D'Oyly Carte Opera Company, which specialized in Gilbert

and Sullivan? You've heard some of the famous songs?"
Ma shook her head.

Mrs. Wilkinson looked as if she might break down
in tears of frustration. I began sympathizing with her
as a little bell jangled in my brain. *D'Oyly Carte.* Of
course! My five desserts worth of information from
Gladys returned: Mrs. Wilkinson's husband had sung
with the company. She had run the chorus. Gilbert
and Sullivan had been her life! Small wonder she was
frustrated.

Mrs. Wilkinson attacked our ignorance with the
piano. She sat down, banged out an introduction
with fingers that sounded more like fists, and sang:

> *"We sail the ocean blue,*
> *And our saucy ship's a beauty;*
> *We're sober men and true,*
> *And attentive to our duty—"*

"Wait!" Ma yelled. "That there's one of my favorite
pieces! You mean to say it's really *opera?*"

"The opening chorus from *H.M.S. Pinafore.*" Mrs.
Wilkinson's lips began to curl into a smile. Other
heads started to nod knowingly.

"I thought *opera* was only for the high muckety-mucks," Kid-Glove Rosie declared. "The ones whose wallets used to fill all my pockets."

An unladylike snort emanated from the corner of the room, from a most unusual source. "Really." Gladys the trustee sniffed in derision. "*I* am quite familiar with the *oeuvres* of Gilbert and Sullivan."

"Well then, why the dickens didn't you say as much, 'stead of letting poor Mrs. Wilkinson get all upset this way?" Ma complained.

Gladys tossed her head.

"And what the devil does that *overs* mean? You could spit it out in plain English like the rest of us."

"I'm not *like* the rest of you!" Gladys snapped back.

"I hope not," Verity said. "A baby killer is the lowest of the low!"

"I just dealt with the results of professions like *yours*," Gladys returned. "A garbage removal service."

A cold hiss passed through the room.

"*You* are the whore here," Verity snarled. "Not the rest of us!"

Gladys sprang—eyes bulging, long manicured fingernails slashing out for Verity's face. It wasn't a pretty sight. My stomach contracted. Another fight.

Another week in our cells. Another seven days without singing. I couldn't stand it.

"*No!* Stop it, Gladys! We can't survive more trouble!"

I lunged as Mrs. Wilkinson spun from her piano stool. We crashed with force and landed in a pile on the floor. Ruby leaned over to offer a tentative hand while Ma dived to the rescue, knocking Ruby into the pile. By the time all the arms and legs and skirts were sorted out, Gladys had disappeared. So had Big Bertha.

Mrs. Wilkinson heaved a sigh of relief. "Gilbert and Sullivan wrote *comic* operas, as I was trying to say. *Comedy*. Something to make us happy. An end devoutly to be desired." She pushed a stray wisp of wavy hair behind an ear. "To digress from the music for only a moment. I know there are already enough rules around Sherborn, but I really and truly believe we need one more new one."

From anyone else this declaration would have brought another sharp hiss. But not from Mrs. Wilkinson. We stared back, waiting for it.

"The new rule, ladies: There'll be NO discussion of anyone's past in this assembly room, or for that matter during any of our rehearsals, no matter where they might be." She stopped. "Do I make myself clear?"

"Clear as crystal, Boss," Ma piped up. "And a good idea, too."

Fifty-four voices agreed in unison. I wasn't the only one who wanted to get on with the most important thing. The music. We all wanted to sing again.

CHAPTER 5

Gladys the Trustee was in solitary detention for seven days. When she emerged at last, her hair no longer glistened. She was also no longer a trustee. Despite the new rule, we'd talked about her during her absence in choir practice. The discussions were lively, and Mrs. Wilkinson took part in them after admitting that rules were made to be bent a little, and anyhow we had to get the subject out of our systems for good and final.

"Killing a no-good husband's one thing," Ma declared, "but what she done . . ."

"Then acting so *superior*—" Rosie added.

"I birthed eleven souls into this world," Ma said pushing back in. "Only five survived—no thanks to Harold—but I loved every single one of 'em to pieces. And would've protected 'em to the death. Didn't I end up with more broken bones than babies?"

Rachel quietly sobbed. "My two little ones were

stillborn. . . . It didn't matter who their fathers were. I *wanted* them. And I would've provided for them. Just see if I wouldn't have!"

"Gladys don't belong in this choir!" Sal declared. "Not if it's supposed to be about *good*."

"Wish I'd known about all this when I was still outside," Molly Matches said. *"There's a house job I would've taken on for no commission whatsoever. It would of been a free-will offering."*

"I was given almost the same sentence as Gladys, and really, there's no relationship between the severity of our actions."

It wasn't one of the regulars speaking. I craned my neck to stare at the neat, gray-haired woman—the kind who usually stood in the background, or slipped between the cracks. The others were staring, too.

"Action?" Ma asked. "What the dickens is a *action?* And if you'll pardon me askin', what might yours've been?"

The quiet woman nodded at Ma. "I'm Dr. Lena Colbrook—" Her voice turned ironic. "The villainous abortionist."

"You—'The Butcher of Boston'!" Rachel began sobbing again.

"The yellow press does enjoy crucifixions to improve its circulation figures. If only they reported their facts accurately."

The doctor's calm voice was hiding unknown worlds, like the ocean. I plunged in. "What were the accurate facts?"

She turned toward me. "I sponsored a birth-control clinic attached to my usual practice. It was a free service. My action, my *crime*, was to save women—women who'd grown old and worn before their time—from giving birth to more babies than they could care for. My *crime* was to attempt to raise women up, freeing them to use their minds rather than their bodies."

Rachel hiccoughed into silence. A few of the girls edged away from Dr. Colbrook, but she interested me. I'd heard about such modern women. I wanted to ask if she was for the vote, too, but Mrs. Wilkinson held up a hand.

"You've given us some food for thought, Dr. Colbrook. Your candor is appreciated. Thanks to all of you for trying to talk this out. I know it's really hard to forget about some past lives—"

"Maybe the doctor lady"—another voice interrupted—"maybe the doctor lady needs a second chance just like the rest of us. Maybe even Gladys does."

We all turned to see where that idea came from. It was Ruby, her voice much stronger than usual.

"Why?" Verity asked. Her sharp-boned face took on that hard look it'd had when she'd tussled with the trustee. She clenched her fists. "Why Gladys? I chose my job to make easy money, but it doesn't hurt anyone. *Her* business did, and she's not a bit sorry."

Mrs. Wilkinson turned between the two speakers, then answered Verity's question. "First, Ruby is right. We *all* deserve a second chance in life. Next—and I'll admit I'm being selfish here—but next, remorseless or not, we *need* Gladys."

Ma humphed, but the chaplain ignored her.

"We need Gladys, because Gladys is the only choir member who could possibly pull off the role of the Major-General—"

"Maybe," I parroted Ruby, "maybe, Mrs. Wilkinson, you ought to tell us a little bit about this *Pirates of Penzance*, so we can figure out the roles for ourselves."

She sighed with relief. "Thank you for reminding us of our real purpose, Libby. *Music.* Try as we might,

I suspect we'll never answer the question of why God allows true evil in the world. We'll also never know if the masks some of us wear hide hideous nightmares. It is time to move forward. And I really feel better about everything when I can hear a little music. I brought the score—" She grabbed for a sheaf of papers sitting atop the upright piano and waved them at us. "Just let me play a few snippets from the main themes. It will put us all in the proper mood for discussing the story itself."

It did. I spread my skirt out on the floor, leaned back, closed my eyes, and listened. Handel had been powerful, but I never thought of music as being happy. As being *funny*. Oh, some of Ma's tunes were silly enough, but that wasn't the same thing. This Gilbert and Sullivan stuff, well, it had charm. And that was even before I learned the words, the *lyrics* that Mr. Gilbert had written to Mr. Sullivan's music. This first time, I just listened, wondering what the story could be like to go with such jaunty music. Wondering what part I would get. Hoping it was a good one. Fighting off jealous thoughts that Gladys would be getting the plum role. When the music stopped at last, I opened my eyes and blinked. Big

Bertha had materialized next to the piano. She towered over Mrs. Wilkinson, who glanced up from the keys.

"What is it, Matron?"

"Time's up."

"Already?"

Big Bertha glowered.

"I don't suppose we could stretch the session for just a few minutes. . . ."

"Mrs. Hodder's orders," growled the matron.

"Ah, yes. Orders. Rules. Where's the place for music?" The chaplain wearily pulled herself up from the stool. "I keep forgetting that this is a prison. Tomorrow, ladies. Tomorrow we'll get to the story. Maybe we'll even get to sing."

By the time Gladys reappeared, the rest of us knew the story of *Pirates of Penzance*. We'd giggled over it as Mrs. Wilkinson walked us through the plot.

"Lemme understand this proper," Ma interrupted. Ma interrupted a lot. The rest of us hardly ever minded, though, because Ma McCreary could always be relied upon to ask the questions most were too shy to ask. Ma never cared about sounding stupid. "As I see it," she went on, "there's these here pirates, but they ain't too successful—"

"Because they're way too tenderhearted!" Second-Story Sal scoffed. "They'd make awful burglars!"

"But that's because they're all *orphans*." Ruby was growing bolder by the day, but she still said this with great sadness. It made me strongly suspect I was not the only orphan within the prison-fortress of Sherborn.

"Also, they're a little randy from being at sea so long," Ma continued, oblivious. "Like my five boys when they gets shore leave. So naturally they'd be hunting up some fine young girlies when they finally hits the land—"

"And who should come along the rocky shore but all these lovely, pretty young ladies—" Verity fingered her tawny hair and her face softened. She had a touch of romance in her soul, I was sure.

"That silly young pirate apprentice Frederic had no idea how to get out of the clutches of the rest of those pirates." Molly Matches was vehement. "Now if he was to have torched the ship, he'd have been away and clean, instead of heading for that cave, and being taken in by the vision of those beauties."

"Why doesn't anybody feel sorry for Ruth?" Flo's voice was plaintive for such a blowzy woman whose years of walking the streets were surely numbered. "She gave the best years of her life to that Frederic as his nursemaid, and now that he's grown the lout wants to dump her. Frederic's not much better than some pimps I could name—"

"Yup, he is a little ungrateful," Ma agreed. "And pretty wet behind the ears, too."

"Your comments are fascinating, ladies," Mrs. Wilkinson broke in. "I'll bet you didn't even know you've been doing character analysis!" She smiled. "It's critical for an actor to learn how to get under the skin of a character. We'll have time to work some more on this analysis after the roles have been assigned. As for plot—"

"*What* plot?" I asked. "The orphan pirates arrive. The Major-General lies about being an orphan to save his nine daughters from marrying the pirates. The pirates decide to attack the Major-General, and the police are called to the rescue. Everyone bumbles around a whole bunch, then the daughters end up marrying the pirates anyhow. This is a plot?"

Mrs. Wilkinson smiled. "No, Libby. This is Gilbert

and Sullivan. Sometimes in life you just have to open your arms wide to the ridiculous. Such is the great gift Gilbert and Sullivan have given us."

"A sense of the absurd is required."

"Ah, Dr. Colbrook." The chaplain squinted in the direction of the dry voice, then fixed on the figure leaning against the far wall. "I wish you'd found your voice a few days ago. Perhaps you'd have been able to help defuse the Gladys incident."

The doctor shrugged at Mrs. Wilkinson. The chaplain stared a moment longer as if trying to understand what made her tick, then turned to her piano.

"We'll begin by warming up our voices with a few scales—"

The room exploded in groans.

"And then we'll move on to *trills*. A trill is a melodic ornament, a sort of embroidery of the note. Gilbert and Sullivan took this ornamentation to almost acrobatic heights." She grinned broadly. "Ladies, you are going to *love* trills."

Gladys, the ex-trustee, lived at the end of my hall in one of those honor cells Ma coveted. I saw her stalking toward it—and me—the evening she got freed from solitary. I wished I could fade into the wall the way Dr. Colbrook did, but no matter how you figured it, Gladys and I had to pass each other. I took a deep breath and decided to make the best of it.

"Good evening, Gladys."

"Libby Dodge."

She made my name sound wicked, stopping me in my tracks.

"Miss Prim-and-Proper herself. Miss Innocence."

"I'm not sure what you mean—"

Gladys hadn't gotten to her shampoo supply yet, and it put her in a temper. Now her temper—and her unwashed body—rammed me against the cold stones of the corridor wall. She pinned me there, so close that I could see the black roots of her blond hair. The sight gave me such a shock that I almost didn't catch the next piece of her diatribe.

"Mrs. Wilkinson's little pet. Too good for the rest of us. But not too good to get me into solitary."

That did it. "You got yourself into solitary. I was only trying to stop a fight! What makes you think—" She was too close. I could feel hives erupting all over my body. "What—" I stuttered, "what—"

"What, indeed. That's the real question, isn't it? What *are* you in Sherborn for, Libby Dodge?"

I stiffened, discomfort forgotten. "That's nobody's business but my own."

"I'll find out!" she spat.

Her breath was pretty mean, too. I tried to give her the benefit of a doubt. I'd never been in solitary confinement myself, but after an entire week of it I suspected a person like Gladys could get a little worked up. She wasn't one to shrink into herself like poor Ruby.

"I'll find out about you just the way I found out about Mrs. Hodder."

"Mrs. Hodder?" I squeaked.

"Our fine, holier-than-thou superintendent. I'll bet you didn't know she's spawned two illegitimate brats herself, from a lover she picked up while studying music in Europe—"

"*Music?*" I squeaked more loudly. The superintendent's two children disappeared. A dozen children would have disappeared. Mrs. Hodder had studied *music?*

"I'll get my trustee job back." Gladys shook me till I focused on her again. "I'll get it back, and then the first file I'll go after is yours!"

"They're locked up. You'll be caught stealing them, Gladys."

She laughed. Threw her head back and laughed. "I don't think so. The superintendent and I have a little agreement." The humor disappeared from her eyes. "At least we used to. But it will soon be reinstated in spades. A little agreement between the two of us—and now you know too, Libby Dodge. It would be dangerous information to share."

Gladys pressed me against the rough stone till I could feel it cutting through the serge of my uniform. I'd had experience with blackmail. Her threat was real. She laughed again.

"Besides, what's a little theft to someone who's a baby killer?"

She backed off, and I tried to make my escape, but her long fingers caught my arm in a viselike grip.

"I didn't murder them, you know. I fed them regularly once a day, whether they were screaming or not. And when they chose to give up—babies can give up just like adults, did you know that, Libby Dodge? When they chose to give up, I buried them nicely. In pretty blankets. Blue for the boys, pink for the girls."

Her grip loosened. I ran.

That night it was a comfort to hear the bolt locking my door. For the first time during my stay at Sherborn it felt as though that bolt wasn't closing me in. It was protecting me. The skin on my back stung as I stripped off my clothing. I ignored it to study my arm. Gladys's sharp fingernails had left red claw marks in the soft skin below the elbow. I rushed for my washcloth and tried to scrub the marks away. Tried to scrub the welts of hives away. Useless. I crawled into bed and dreamed of long rows of babies screaming from hunger.

Gladys showed up at choir practice the next afternoon. Her hair was shining and thick again—and blond clear down to the scalp. She must have spent all night tending to it in her cell's tiny washbowl. Her fingernails were newly polished. Her mask was in place again. Everything back in place, as if nothing had ever happened. Maybe it hadn't. Maybe I'd dreamed about the encounter in the corridor, dreamed about Mrs. Hodder's past. I'd leave it there forever. The superintendent's need for privacy might be as keen as mine. I glanced away from Gladys quickly, but not quickly enough. Little pink and blue blankets began swirling through my head again. I fought down the urge to scratch my arms, my legs.

Everyone else was being properly Christian. Mrs. Wilkinson's sweet sermons were all fine and good, yet it was those few words from Ruby that really made the difference for the others. People did need a second chance. It was true. But was Gladys really human?

It rained. Hard, chill end-of-April showers that made it impossible to work in the garden. On such days, Sparky allowed us entry to his inner sanctum. This was the glassed-in greenhouse where he babied the plants that couldn't be set out in the tricky New England weather until at least late May. He'd shepherd the crew through the door, then watch anxiously as we edged down the narrow main aisle. Rows of potted plants were balanced precariously on shaky tables to either side. A pot-bellied stove and chair waited at the far end.

"Don't be bumbling into any of my tomatoes, Belle McCreary!"

"I knows a tomato plant when I sees one, Sparky O'Connor! You think I was born on the other side, like you, where nothing grows but potatoes?"

"The old country's not to be faulted for its climate, woman—"

"Excuse me, Sparky," I interrupted. These two

would argue forever otherwise. "What's this?" I pointed at a plant with slim, smooth leaves.

"Oh, aye, that'd be a pepper." He pulled out his pipe and set to stuffing it, a process which always calmed him considerably. A match, a few puffs, and he was off again. "See, Libby girl, there be two kinds of peppers here. This one makes the big, dark-green bell kind"—he clumped down a few feet—"and this makes long, thin, yellow peppers."

I pointed again. "And this?"

"Eggplant," he grinned. "Now that's something you'd never find in the old country for sure—"

"Depends which old country you mean," Emma spoke up. "My mama's from Italy, and you never tasted anything like her eggplant parmigiana done up in tomato sauce and cheese."

Sparky puffed at his pipe, considering. "Sliced and fried in a little oil, mebbe, but eggplant and tomato?"

"You startin' a cooking school or what, Sparky?" Ma complained. "If we can't eat it, I don't want to be talkin' about it. Oatmeal, hard rolls, and tough stew meat is beginning to grate on me."

"Should've given a thought to that before you done the whacking, Belle."

Ma humphed mightily, and Sparky finally got down to business. "Some of the babies're outgrowing their homes. Today I mean to teach you how to repot a plant proper."

That was fine with me. I'd gotten to enjoy the feel of soil between my fingers. Lucky, too, because soon I was up to my elbows in it, learning which plants were given a little potassium, which ones just needed a handful of dried cow manure mixed into their pots. It was a soothing morning after the recent drama in my life. And it gave me time to think about Gilbert and Sullivan, too.

This was to be the big day. The day when Mrs. Wilkinson would announce her choices for the leading roles in the *Pirates of Penzance*. I supposed I had a chance at one of Major-General Stanley's nine daughters, yet which one? Edith, Kate, and Isabel all had a few speaking lines, and a few modest solos as well . . . but *Mabel*. I'd almost trade another month in Sherborn to get the role of Mabel. The ingenue role. Frederic's love interest.

Oh, I'd seen a little theatre on Washington Street in Boston myself. But it wasn't to Ma's vaudeville houses that I'd gone. It was the plays that called to me. I would sneak off for an afternoon matinee of the latest romantic drama. Plays where the wronged young lady—the ingenue—was always avenged in the last scene. Her besmirched reputation was cleared. She got to marry the handsome hero—*and* live happily ever after.

"*Ouch!*"

"What is it, Libby?"

"Nothing, Ma. I wasn't paying attention and pricked myself on a sharp tine of Sparky's potting fork." I sucked at my finger. Pricked my balloon full of silly dreams, too.

The whole choir was giddy again, this time with excitement. We buzzed around the assembly room, bombarding each other with trills that became ever more elaborate, ever more shrill. Mrs. Wilkinson tried to get our attention and make us settle down, but we were having none of it. I'd just raised my voice an entire octave to crush Second-Story Sal's alto, when the chaplain held up her conducting hand. This time it gripped a little stick. She cleared her throat. Vigorously. The trilling faded to a few squeaks.

"Ladies." Mrs. Wilkinson made a firm attempt at

sternness. "Let's make one thing absolutely clear before we embark on our great endeavor. When I raise my conducting hand, I expect total and absolute attention. Conducting is generalship on the battle-field of music. *I* am the general. *You* are the troops. And this object"—she waved the stick—"this *baton* gives the orders. With the baton I will set the tempo."

She demonstrated by tapping out a two beat, then a four beat.

"You'll learn to follow the baton's movements to work up to a crescendo. . . . But more to the point, the baton will also tell you when to stop. When I want complete and instant silence, like this." She thrashed the baton like a whip. "Do you follow?"

"How come you didn't play general with that there stick on Easter Sunday?" Ma wanted to know.

Mrs. Wilkinson sighed. "Because on Easter Sunday I didn't own a baton. It only arrived this morning. A gift from one of our Easter guests. They also kindly donated a metronome—" She caught Ma's question before it could be spit out. "A *metronome*, Mrs. McCreary, is this object."

She reached for a small, pyramid-shaped box sit-ting atop the piano. Next she pulled out a rod, gave it a nudge, and it began to swing back and forth, very fast, like a drunken, upside-down pendulum. Fifty-five sets of eyes darted back and forth with the rod in time with its ticks till Mrs. Wilkinson popped it back into its case.

"As you see, a metronome also keeps tempo, and can be set to different beats. It's a device most useful for keeping up a musician's—or vocalist's—speed."

Ma's head was still going back and forth. "Lord. That'll get us so dizzy, we'll be fainting all over the floor. Why can't we just go back to the pianner and your hand, 'stead of fussing with these new toys?"

Mrs. Wilksinson sighed again. "We will, but we also want to go about our show like professionals—"

I raised my hand for attention.

"Yes, Libby?"

"Excuse me, but if your hands are going to be busy with the baton, being our general, who's going to play the piano?"

Mrs. Wilkinson took a step back, as if the thought hadn't occurred to her.

"I mean, one-handed is fine for our rehearsals, but for the finished show, we're going to need both hands' worth of music—"

"Libby's right." Ma gave me a proud look. "I always knew she was a clever girl. You're gonna need three hands, Boss."

Gladys made a sound of disgust before Lena Colbrook pushed away from her wall.

"Yes, Doctor?" Mrs. Wilkinson sounded as if she were reaching for a life preserver.

"My voice isn't as strong as some of the other women's," the doctor admitted. "So my absence from the chorus would not be a loss. But I can read music and play the piano. Perhaps if I were to study the score with you. . . ?"

Relief burst over the chaplain. "Thank you, Dr. Colbrook. If you'd speak to me after our rehearsal?" She turned to the rest of us. With fresh confidence her conducting baton crashed into her palm. "Now for the moment I believe you've been anticipating— the *cast*."

The murmur rose from every throat.

"You're going to pick the cast!"

"I *have* picked the cast." Mrs. Wilkinson reached into a pocket and pulled out a slip of paper. She cleared her throat, but it wasn't necessary. She had our complete attention.

"Let me preface this by saying once more that our production of the *Pirates of Penzance* will be a team effort."

The little piece of paper stood stiffly in her fingers. I wished for X-ray eyes to read straight through to the other side. It didn't do a bit of good. Mrs. Wilkinson only kept raising the tension.

"*All* of you are critical to our final success. *All* of you will have the opportunity to sing your hearts out—"

"*All* of us ain't going to live as long as it takes you to spill the news!" Ma fussed.

Mrs. Wilkinson started giving Ma a look, then her face changed in mid-expression. She laughed. "*All* of you probably feel the same way! Well, then, here goes."

She started at the top.

"Major-General Stanley: Gladys."

Silence. It wasn't a surprise to any of us, except for Gladys—and she just put a hand to her mouth in shock, then straightened her shoulders and tossed her head.

"The Pirate King," Mrs. Wilkinson continued, "will be performed by"—she glanced up—"Mrs. Belle McCreary."

Ma whooped. So did everyone else. She was a good choice. A popular choice.

"Samuel, his lieutenant: Second-Story Sal." Mrs. Wilkinson speeded up over the applause. "Frederic, the Pirate Apprentice: Verity."

Verity pumped a victory fist.

"The Sergeant of Police," Mrs. Wilkinson continued. "Kid-Glove Rosie."

Rosie roared with laughter. "Me, head of the police! I'll get my revenge on them coppers for once!"

Mrs. Wilkinson paused to let the general commotion simmer down. "Now for Major-General Stanley's daughters . . ."

A bunch of us hopefuls pushed closer.

"Kate, Molly Matches; Isabel, Rachel; Edith—" She stopped to smile. "Edith will be played by Ruby."

All eyes fell on the young woman. She still huddled within the protection of her arms, but her hair had gone from a stringy mess to soft chestnut waves pinned loosely about her heart-shaped face. Her complexion had begun to take on a little color in the last few weeks, too.

"Me?" Ruby asked.

"Yes, you," Mrs. Wilkinson answered.

Tears slid down Ruby's face. "Nothing . . . no one . . . never . . . Nobody ever gave me a chance before."

"I'm giving you a chance, Ruby."

Well, then the next two roles almost seemed like an afterthought. I held my breath anyway.

"Ruth, a Pirate Maid of all Work: Florence." Mrs. Wilkinson looked up from the sheet of paper. "Because I do believe you've got a true feeling for her character, Flo. . . . And last, but not least, the role of Mabel will be performed by Libby Dodge."

The breath sighed right out of me. I sank back trying to find it again, then Ma inched over to give me a good solid thwack on the back. "Ain't that just the berries!"

I found my breath again. "You took the words right out of my mouth, Ma."

The casting of pirates and policemen came next, and the remainder of the rehearsal became a joyous shambles as the Sherborn Choir turned it into a dance, with Mrs. Wilkinson pounding out Gilbert and Sullivan's music on the old upright piano. Even Big Bertha couldn't put a crimp in our party.

CHAPTER 7

"**O**ooh."

I woke up a few mornings later to rain. Again. I matched the day. Achy. Stiff. More than under the weather. When I tried to pull off my nightgown, I groaned again as the cloth caught my left hand. My left hand? I opened my eyes properly to inspect it. What a sight! The finger I'd pricked in the greenhouse was swollen, and little red lines were creeping up my palm like crooked roads. I stared at the map in grim fascination until I heard the bolt slide open on my door.

"Wait!"

Yanking the nightgown back in place, I rushed to the door to catch the matron. Stuck my hand in her face.

"Infirmary," she ordered, and continued on down the line.

*　　*　　*

I made my way in nightclothes along the suddenly endless dormitory corridor, past the work block with its laundry and sewing room, and finally into the farthest wing. This was a place I'd never been before, a journey of miles. I suddenly realized my feet were bare and freezing from the cold stone slabs of the floor. The rest of me felt hot. By the time I stumbled over the infirmary's threshold, I was slick with sweat. I stood there a moment frowning at lined-up rows of empty beds: soldiers neatly dressed in uniforms of fresh white linen. Then I collapsed.

"Libby? Libby."

A soft, calm voice was calling to me. Not really familiar, yet . . .

"Libby."

I tried to open my eyes. "Where am I? Who—"

"You're in the infirmary, my dear. With a kind of blood poisoning."

"What!" I tried to sit up, only to fall weakly into the pillows again. Then I really opened my eyes. "Dr. Colbrook?" It was an effort getting the words out of my throat. It felt so tight. "What . . . are you doing here?"

"Where else should I be serving my work time, Libby? Superintendent Hodder kindly agreed that I could be of no harm to the women here. I am—first and foremost—a healer, after all."

I blinked. "But . . ." Why was my jaw so stiff? "What happened to me?"

"Your finger became infected. I do need to ask how it might have happened."

"Oh." It came back. "Sparky's sharp potting fork . . . in the greenhouse . . . pricked myself . . ."

"Listen carefully, young lady. Was it rusty?"

I tried to think. That was hard, too. A little jerk ran through my body. What was it . . . ? Yes, Sparky's tools. Mostly handmade and makeshift. "Prob—" Another spasm. "Probably rusty."

"His tools will have to be destroyed."

"Poor Sparky . . . upset—"

"Poor Sparky will be killing himself—and others—with his rusty implements if he's not more careful."

I almost giggled. "Ma—Mrs. McCreary—wouldn't be the only murderer then . . . would she?" I sobered and shifted to try to study my injured hand. It was wrapped up to the elbow in something smelly. "But it was just . . . a little puncture. How could this be?"

"Tetanus," the doctor explained. "It attacks the nerves as well as the blood."

Tetanus. That surely sounded evil. Something familiar about it, too. I bolted upright. "You mean *lockjaw?* People . . . *die* of lockjaw! I'm not ready to die! I've . . . got to be Mabel!"

Dr. Colbrook reached her hand across the bed to cup my chin. It was comforting. Then she efficiently pounded life into my flattened pillows and eased me back into them.

"Try to settle yourself, Libby. I'm going to give you some medicine—really not much more than a country remedy for the moment. We can at least attempt to subdue the inflammation and allay the muscle spasms while we wait. Mrs. Hodder has sent a special messenger to Boston to fetch the antitoxin. We'll go with the old ways until it arrives."

The doctor presented a large soup spoon filled with a disgusting mess. I felt my face contort into a grimace.

"It's not that bad! Merely an antispasmodic tincture with calcium, laudanum, and a lot of herbs—which is what the medicine cabinet seems to hold. I don't believe the infirmary has been restocked since the prison was built forty years ago." She shrugged. "Please be a good girl and swallow it all. We've got to wage war against the *Clostridium tetani* bacillus."

War? It was too much to understand. I swallowed what she offered and slumped back into a listless doze broken every few minutes by more of those spasms. Maybe it was the laudanum, because when my body stilled enough for real sleep, the dreams arrived.

I was in the greenhouse again. The plant I was trying to repot kept growing. Larger and larger it grew right before my eyes. No sooner had I settled it in a new home, when I had to begin the labor all over again. When I looked up from the fourth pot, a huge, leafy, green monster was leering down at me.

"Sparky!" I cried. "Sparky! What's this one?"

He hobbled over and inspected it between puffs of his pipe. "That'd be an uncommon one, dearie. A *Clostridium tetani*. Be good to it, eh?"

"Be good to it? Sparky! It's going to *eat* me!"

"The *Clostridium tetani* has a rare appetite, it does."

"Sparky!" My pleas did no good. In desperation I called for the one person who could help. "Ma! Ma! Save me! Ma . . ."

"Hush, Libby girl. I'm right here. In the flesh."

"Ma?" My whole body jerked, long and hard. When I got control of it again, my good hand was clutching at the white sheets. The room was almost dark. "What . . . time is it?" My words still came hard. And there were so many I wanted to say. "Choir . . . practice?"

"Got myself excused. Been here the livelong afternoon, helping the doc feed you that horrible stuff every ten minutes."

"But . . . but *Mabel*—"

"Mrs. Wilkinson says not to fret. Just get yourself well. The part'll be waitin' for you."

"Boston?" I tried. "Anti . . . toxin?"

"Been some problems trackin' it down. Ain't all that easy to find, you know. Might have to ship some by train from New York. But it'll be here tomorrow, for sure and certain."

Now someone else hovered behind Mother McCreary. She pushed into view. The doctor.

"It's time for me to change that poultice, Mrs. McCreary. And reheat the bricks for Libby's feet and legs. Maybe you'd better be going to supper before you miss it."

"Missing my supper ain't important noways. I'm stickin' right here till my girl's out of this fix. In the meantime, I can be helping you with the wrapping of those bricks. In vinegar-soaked cloth, kee-rect?"

"Kee—correct."

Ma gave my good hand a squeeze. "Hang on, girl. I'll be spendin' the night if I have to get down on my knees to the superintendent and beg."

"Thank . . . Thank you. . . ."

The antitoxin arrived the next morning. Mrs. Hodder herself arrived with it. I woke long enough to catch the conversation as she handed the package to Dr. Colbrook.

"I had to go directly to the governor to clear this, Dr. Colbrook. Mountains were moved. I hope the inmate is worth it."

Lena Colbrook smiled. "From what I've observed, and from what Mrs. Wilkinson implies, the young lady is absolutely worth it. Now, I need to administer this as quickly as possible. Next, she'll require complete rest and quiet for a few days."

"And then?" asked the superintendent.

"Then we shall see if the cure works."

I drifted off again, even though I fought sleep. The dreams always became the same nightmare, except that *Clostridium tetani* kept growing. Something new was added to the plot, though. Off in the distance, beyond all the threatening foliage, I could begin to see the glimmer of flashing swords as a horde of pirates, led by a splendid Pirate King, came slashing to the rescue.

"Libby Dodge." The whisper was right next to my ear. "Listen to me. I snuck in. Against the rules. But I had to tell you. Had to help you."

My eyes felt glued shut. I couldn't open them, could only listen as ordered. The whisper began again.

"You ain't like me. You're different somehow. I seen you staring at me, but not like the others. You stare the way Mrs. Wilkinson does, with kindness in your heart. But that's not what I need to say—" A gulp and a little sob, then more. "What I need to say is, watch careful they don't feed you too much of that laudanum. It was my downfall. Laudanum. And morphine. Next it'll be *opium*. Then you're for solitary, too. That's how they give us dope fiends the cure. Jail us, and throw us in solitary. And it hurts so bad, Libby Dodge. Nobody knows how bad it hurts when they take it away. . . ." The voice halted as a clanking sound echoed through the distance. *"Remember."*

I drifted back into my nightmare.

There was another interruption of the never-ending dream. This one had no voice—only cool fingers that hovered over my good hand. They settled atop it briefly, then disappeared.

"Libby?"

My eyes opened at last, and my words came more easily. "Mrs. Wilkinson!"

"It's morning again. How do you feel?"

"Which morning?"

"You are a clever girl, just as Mrs. McCreary keeps insisting."

I glanced around. I'd been moved to a bed next to a window. On its sill stood a jug stuffed with a collection of wildflowers. Their colors were bright, bursting with life. "Did Ma bring these?"

The chaplain shook her head. "They just appeared."

"Where is she? Ma?"

"Getting some hard-earned sleep. We've taken turns keeping vigil with you these past four days."

"Four days!" I sat up. "*Oooh.*"

She gently pushed me back. "Don't force yourself yet."

"But Gilbert and Sullivan!"

"We've moved forward with the rehearsals in your absence, Libby. We had to. But I've been working with the chorus members. You won't have missed anything when you return."

I inched up more tentatively. "When will that be?"

"Your progress is promising. A few more days."

I sank back. "I can't return to the greenhouse. The nightmares . . ." They terrified me. Another idea edging around the corners of my mind was beginning to terrify me, too. The cool fingers had not been threatening—but that whispered voice. Had I dreamed it? Or had it been real? All this laudanum being pressed on me. Laudanum . . . morphine. Next, *opium*. Ruby? Who else could whisper that way? Who else was so intimate with solitary confinement? "Please. No more laudanum. No more greenhouse. I'm scared."

Mrs. Wilkinson considered my words carefully.

"As for the drugs, I'll take that up with Dr. Colbrook. And the greenhouse? You won't be going back to garden duty at all, Libby. You'll be unsuited for heavy labor for quite some time. Superintendent Hodder felt that during your recuperation you'd be most useful as my special assistant." She smiled. "A real one this time."

I motioned toward my bad hand, still packaged to the elbow in a reeking poultice. "How can I help like this?"

"I'll be needing copies of the lyrics written out for all the choir members. And your right hand, your writing hand, will be quite useful enough."

"Ah . . . Thank you."

I closed my eyes and thanked heaven she'd chosen me as her pet.

CHAPTER 6

I never expected my cell to feel like home, but that's what happened when Dr. Colbrook finally released me from the infirmary. The mysterious bouquet of wildflowers had cheered my spirits till they'd faded. Studying them for hours—peridot-blue bachelor buttons, and real golden daisies rather than the silk ones trimming the hat I still missed—I'd discovered a hunger for growing things almost as strong as my yearning for music. I went straight to my geranium, suddenly afraid that it would be wilting, or even dead without my constant attention. But the earth around the roots was moist—not too moist, just enough— and two new stems of flowers had opened to smile on me. "Ma did this, too," I whispered to the plant. "She's the best friend I've ever had." I considered, then added, "Maybe Mrs. Wilkinson is one, too. And Ruby . . . Maybe I've got more friends than I ever thought to have."

It was time to meet Mrs. Wilkinson in the library for my new duties. I opened the window to air my home, adjusted the sling cradling my left arm, and set off down the corridor.

I hadn't spent much time in the library. There never seemed to be much reason to spend time there. I walked in and inspected it again. It was a medium-size room with several heavy tables and chairs sprinkled around, and a large, gloomy, unwelcoming painting called "Christ and the Erring Woman" centered on one wall. Around the painting were built-in shelves.

I guess I'd never spent much time here because of what the shelves held: rows of tattered hymnals and Bibles, and not much else. I'd filled chapel hours with these, but I longed for something a little more entertaining—just a few novels would be a refreshing distraction for those moments before lights out. Moments when you wanted to think about anything but another night alone with your sins in Sherborn.

Mrs. Wilkinson glanced up from the table where she'd spread out piles of papers.

"There you are, Libby! You are looking better. I'll try not to overtire you today, but the choir is getting anxious for their parts. Look here—" She gestured toward the papers. "I've got the libretto separated into sheets and have been trying to decide how best to go about our business. We'll start with the opening chorus, but it's so complicated, I'm becoming quite frightened with what I've taken on."

I leaned over to read the first few lines.

Pour, O pour the pirate sherry;
Fill, O fill the pirate glass—

I looked up. "What's so hard about that, Mrs. Wilkinson?"

"Nothing, if you merely read them as simple words. But I'd like to do the show with the proper British accents—"

"Everyone is going to have to learn accents on top of the words and tunes?"

"You see my problem." She patted the adjoining chair. "Sit down, Libby. Now these first two lines: there's nothing unusual there except the last word, *glass*. In order to enjoy Gilbert's rhyme, it needs to be pronounced 'gloss.'"

"Why?"

"Because two lines later, it needs to rhyme with,

"And, to make us more than merry
Let the pirate bumper pass.

"'Poss' is how they'd say 'pass.'"

A little pain shot through my mending arm. "I guess *bumper* means glass, too. It's like learning another language. This is going to be tricky."

"Which is why I haven't even considered scheduling our performance until late summer at the earliest."

"Halloween might be better."

We both sort of chuckled over that, then I had an idea. "When I copy out the words, Mrs. Wilkinson, why don't I copy down the tricky ones the way they're supposed to sound, instead of the way they should be properly spelled?"

The chaplain stared at me. "My dear, that's a brilliant solution!" As if a weight had been shoved from her shoulders, she began to bubble. "I'll just work through each section with you. We can decide on the diacritical and orthographic symbols to use—" She stopped at the look on my face. "On second thought, phonetic spellings as you suggested will probably be sufficient."

"Good." My vaunted education had a few gaps.

"Let's get busy, then, shall we? We'll certainly have fun with Ruth—Frederic's nursemaid and the Pirate Maid of all Work's—first solo, when she's playing with *pilot* versus *pirate*. Gilbert did so enjoy toying with his words!"

Mrs. Wilkinson and I had forgotten one little thing. We remembered it fast enough when I began handing around my carefully copied lines to the pirate chorus during the afternoon's practice. I got a few excited smiles, several short expressions of thanks, and selected silences. Embarrassed silences. It took me longer than it should have to figure out the cause. It was only when I saw my pages held upside down in Emma's hands that I caught on. I turned the sheet right side up.

"It goes this way, Emma."

"Thank you, Libby."

The choir was clustered in small groups around the assembly room, and we were off to one side by ourselves. I wasn't sure how to do so, but it had to be verified. I finally went for the direct approach.

"You can't read, can you, Emma?"

"Oh, Libby!" Tears popped from the corners of her eyes. "Libby! I want to be a pirate so bad, and I'll lose my place! What'll I do?"

"Didn't you even go to baby school, Emma?"

She shook her head. "Never had shoes to go to it in. There was only enough money to dress up the boys right. My mama was shamed and kept me home, learning how to cook. Then the first time I snuck out and got myself in trouble, Papa kicked me out for good." She was sniffling in earnest by this time. "And who needs to read and write when you make your living flat on your back?"

"Oh, Emma. Emma." I couldn't think of what else to say. At least I hadn't ended flat on my back. But I'd never had her years of eggplant parmigiana, either. My arm twinged mightily. "Listen, it's not the end of the world. I have some extra time now. I'll go over the lines with you. You can memorize them the right way."

"Would you?"

We'd begun to attract attention. Soon there were another half dozen choir members with the same problem surrounding us. Then Mrs. Wilkinson noticed and walked over.

"Illiterate! All of you?" She turned suddenly fierce. "Well, there's a dirty word that *will* be eliminated if I have anything to say about it!"

The rest of May sped past. Sherborn hummed again, but this time it was to the sounds of Gilbert and Sullivan rather than Handel. After breakfast each morning I rushed to the library to copy out the next set of lyrics necessary for the afternoon's practice. I would barely accomplish the task before Emma and her friends arrived for their reading lessons before lunch. No one expected them to actually be able to read in time for rehearsals and the performance. Learning lines would still be accomplished by memorization. When our chaplain got a bee in her bonnet, though, there was no stopping the woman. Mrs. Jessie D. Hodder had been properly shamed into approving Sherborn's new literacy program.

Dr. Colbrook was officially in charge of these lessons now that her infirmary was vacant. Mrs. Wilkinson would pop in, and I was allowed to stick around and help because a few minutes before and after class were saved for my *Pirates of Penzance* memorization drills.

While it was true that the superintendent had been coerced, she still held the upper hand: Dr. Colbrook was required to use the Bible as a reading text. Well, anyone who's ever had a look at the Bible has to know that it's pretty hard. Once you get past the first sentence in the first chapter of Genesis, the words only become tougher and tougher. But Dr. Colbrook had a system. She concentrated on that first sentence.

Mrs. Wilkinson begged a blackboard and chalk from somewhere. I directed Emma and Rachel to neatly position the blackboard to hide the "Erring Woman" painting, and wrote out the verse in big block letters:

IN THE BEGINNING,

GOD CREATED THE HEAVEN AND THE EARTH.

Now it was the doctor's turn. She pulled out all the letters and showed how they sounded by themselves, and how they sounded when you made a word from them.

That first day, the new literacy students went to lunch with homework clutched in their hands. They

had to memorize all twenty-six letters of the alpha-
bet, even though they hadn't met all of those letters
yet in that first sentence. And this was on top of the
Gilbert and Sullivan chores I'd given them. They
looked fairly frazzled.

After lunch I was required to rest for several hours
before attending to other errands for the show.
Doctor's orders. But as I began feeling much better, I
started wandering into the assembly room instead of
my cell. I'd curl up in a back corner and listen to Lena
Colbrook practice the score for *Pirates of Penzance*. She
was beginning to sound almost as good at it as Mrs.
Wilkinson. I'd nod off a little, then jerk awake to different sounds.

"Doctor?" I ambled up to the piano. "That's not
Gilbert and Sullivan anymore, is it?"

"No, Libby. This is Chopin, the poet of the piano.
One of his études."

"Oh. He's . . . it's lovely."

"I think so, too."

Big Bertha poked her head through the door, making her usual body count. The doctor's fingers slipped
seamlessly from Chopin into Mabel's first solo. On
cue, I sang,

"Poor wandering one!

Though thou hast surely strayed,

Take heart of grace,

Thy steps retrace,

Poor wandering one!"

After half a verse, Bertha nodded stern approval of the sentiment. Then she was gone, and Chopin was back again. I sank gratefully to the floor next to the instrument, closed my eyes, and let Chopin's music sweep me away. Lena Colbrook's fingers never hesitated over these notes. She poured into them emotions I'd never have suspected her of having. Gone were the dryness, the self-deprecation. What emerged were fire and passion.

Could I ever give Mabel that kind of passion? Did I have that much passion within me? So many things to learn. Music was much more than Handel, or Gilbert and Sullivan. It held whole entire worlds. People were the same. Who would think Big Bertha could endorse Mabel's solo? Who would think Dr. Lena Colbrook could carry within her medicine, and music, and convictions strong enough to land her in prison? Who would ever know, looking at her quiet, graying figure—if they'd never heard her play?

The music ended quietly, the last notes of the Chopin reverberating through the empty room. I looked up.

"Isn't it time for your afternoon rounds, Libby?"

"Yes. Thank you for reminding me." Cradling my left arm I struggled up, then paused at the door. "Tomorrow, Dr. Colbrook . . . Will you play more Chopin tomorrow?"

The tight lines around her mouth softened. "Perhaps I'll introduce you to Mozart, instead. Or maybe even Beethoven."

"I'd like that. Very much."

COSTUME DEPARTMENT! I smiled at the sign. It had brightened every single day for me since the sewing ladies installed the huge sheet with its painted letters on the wall next to the machine room. They were taking their role in the production of *The Pirates of Penzance* as seriously as the choir. Nothing could be better. I marched in.

"Afternoon, all. Is the costume mistress about?"

"Libby!" The Swindling Snodgrass Twins stopped treadling their machines in unison.

"Agnes has been waiting for you."

"She's off counting those bolts of cloth again."

They both pointed toward the rear of the enormous, factory-size room.

"Thanks, Fanny. Thanks, Freda." I trotted off in search of Agnes Cordoni past dozens of clattering machines illuminated by sunlight streaming through tall, regularly placed windows.

"You're late, Libby!" she popped from behind the mountain of cloth. "A stage manager should always be on time!"

I almost glanced around for somebody else. Mrs. Wilkinson had upgraded me from assistant, and I wasn't yet used to the title change. "Sorry, Agnes, I got caught in a music consultation with Dr. Colbrook."

"Well, since you're here at last, we need to have a serious talk." She pointed at the bolts. "This is what we've got to work with at the moment. About a hundred years' worth of navy blue serge, and the same of white duck."

"But," I allowed, "Sherborn has never needed anything but uniforms and aprons before—"

Agnes plowed right on. "Work with what we've

got, Mrs. Wilkinson says. All fine and good for the pirates' pants and shirts and the policemen's uniforms, but what happens when we have to produce lovely frocks for all those daughters of Major-General Stanley? What then, Libby Dodge?"

Mildred was eavesdropping from the nearest machine. She raised her voice over the din. "Why don't we send Second-Story Sal and Kid-Glove Rosie over the wall for a little foraging? They'd come back with the goods!"

"Umm." It was really hard trying to keep a straight face. "I'm sure they would, Mildred, but—"

"And while they're at it, I could use some head blocks and felt, too. How'm I expected to create hats from nothing?"

"The measurements," Agnes broke in. "We've got to begin taking measurements at once. At least for the pirates and policemen. Then we can get started on those costumes and continue with the fittings as they progress. Another thing—"

I grinned. Here was an Agnes unrecognizable from the harridan who'd almost destroyed my precious button-top shoes that long-ago September day. I waited for her demands to grind to a halt.

"I've got great news about all of that, Agnes. Get your tailoring gear collected, because starting tonight, you'll be able to begin taking those measurements. We're back on the Handel schedule before lights out—" I suddenly noticed all the sewing machines had stopped. Everyone was raptly following the conversation.

"The Handel schedule? Rehearsals every night?"

"*Hallelujah!*"

So that's how our evening rehearsals came to be called "The Hallelujah Hour."

CHAPTER 9

The first Hallelujah Hour was total chaos. The entire costume department had come armed with measuring tapes and pins and even bolts of cloth and expected to be the center of attention. The chorus did try to give them their wish. Pirates shoved past policemen to be at the head of the line. This was totally in character for pirates and to be expected. Policemen forcefully shoved back, which unfortunately was also in character. Mrs. Wilkinson took on a hunted look and pulled at tufts of her hair. Circling behind her, Big Bertha and her fellow matrons drew in their breaths and thrust out their formidable bosoms, itching for a fight. They were the only ones unhappy with the resumption of late rehearsals. It kept most of them longer at their jobs.

At last Mrs. Wilkinson gathered the presence of mind to raise her baton and bring it crashing down. The choir turned to stone. The costume department put two and two together and followed suit.

"Thank you, ladies." Mrs. Wilkinson ran a sleeve across her brow. June was fast approaching and the evening was unusually warm. But not that warm. "Now, let's do try and get some organization into our endeavors, shall we? Dr. Colbrook, if I may have your assistance—"

The doctor emerged from the fray. "Yes?"

"Kindly take the Major-General's daughters to the piano and rehearse their entrance number, 'Climbing over Rocky Mountain.'"

Lena Colbrook nodded and all nine of the Major-General's daughters—including me—gathered around the piano. As the doctor hunted for the correct place in the score, I watched Mrs. Wilkinson continue her structuring attempts.

"Where is our costume mistress? Ah, Agnes. I believe we need more than one line. Many more lines. Set up your ladies in teams of three or four, please. Pirates? Queue up for measurements before the first three teams—" She stopped. "What seems to be the problem, Mrs. McCreary?"

"That there letter Q is what," Ma answered, hands on hips.

"It's a Britishism, Mrs. McCreary. Start getting

used to them. We are performing a *British* opera." Mrs. Wilkinson softened the edge in her voice. "It means the same thing as *line up*."

"Oh, all right then," Ma conceded.

"Policemen?" the chaplain continued. "*Queue* up in front of the final wardrobe teams."

A shuffling sort of order commenced.

"That's right. Good . . . anyone not involved with the singing or costuming, kindly seat yourself to the rear with your needlework and observe our silence rule."

One of the kitchen workers raised her hand. "Please, Mrs. Wilkinson, ma'am. Ain't us cooks and scullery maids going to get to help with the play, too?"

"Yes, Mary, of course you are. But your help comes a little later along."

"Please, ma'am," Mary insisted. "How?"

Mrs. Wilkinson stood dumb, obviously not yet having thought things through to that point. Meanwhile, Dr. Colbrook had finally located her spot in the music and had hands raised to begin. I glanced at the words I already knew. All the daughters were traipsing across the rocky shore on a little holiday walk. I imagined the scene in my mind. "Mrs. Wilkinson?"

"What is it, Libby?" Her weariness came through.

"Now that we've actually started in with my role as Mabel, I'm going to be pretty busy singing—"

"Yes?" It was a get-to-the-point sort of *yes*. Dr. Colbrook's fingers were still poised over the keys, frozen. The entire room was listening with interest.

"Well, I'm also stage manager." I paused. "And I'm going to need some help with that. A lot of help, in fact. Do you think Mary and everyone else not singing or sewing could help me work on the set design? We're going to need at least a part of a pirate ship built, and some rocky shores, and—"

"Bless my soul!" Mary lit up. Her friends from the kitchen did, too. "It'll be so much fun building something besides bread and rolls!"

"And painting, too!" another woman added. "If I can do icing on a cake, I don't see why I couldn't paint these here ships and rocks, too!"

Chaos broke out again. Down came Mrs. Wilkinson's baton of generalship. "Ladies, please!"

Silence.

"First, thank you, Libby, for the excellent suggestion. Mary, I'm officially placing you in charge of set design. I want some ideas on paper by the end of the week." She stared across the horde of inmates. "Now may we proceed?"

We did proceed:

> "Climbing over rocky mountain,
> Skipping rivulet and fountain,
> Passing where the willows quiver,
> By the ever-rolling river,
> Swollen with the summer rain . . ."

And by the end of the week, across the entrance to the kitchen a banner floated large enough to rival that of the sewing shop: SET DEPARTMENT!!

The third week in June I threw away my sling. My arm still twinged now and again, but the swelling and the road map were long gone. It was an incredible relief. I'd begun to worry about actually having to play the role of Mabel with the sling thrown over the shoulder of a gorgeous dress. It was not a pretty image in my mind. The sling, that is. The gown I imagined was something else. It was an extravaganza of organdy and white lawn to set off my flowing black locks, with maybe a sash of garnet-hued satin—or perhaps sapphire, to bring out the color of my eyes. There'd be a parasol to twirl. Of course there'd be. Not to mention a fantastic hat studded with flowers and fruit and the most exotic of plumes.

All, alas, a pipe dream. The production still hadn't progressed past those bolts of navy blue serge. It was beginning to worry me so much that my pen nib caught of its own accord on the paper of the copy I was making one morning, splattering ink all over my careful script.

"Drat!"

"What is it, Libby?" Mrs. Wilkinson shoved a pair of gold-rimmed spectacles higher up on her nose. She'd taken to wearing them lately for close work.

"I've just ruined this entire second verse of the Major-General's song. And it's the tough one, too. The one where he rhymes 'differential calculus' with 'beings animalculous.'" I tossed the sheet aside in a fit of despair.

Mrs. Wilkinson removed the spectacles and pinched the ridge of her nose. "It hardly matters. Gladys has most of the lyrics memorized already anyway. What is it that's really troubling you, Libby?"

"The costumes!" I exclaimed. "We still need decent costumes for all the leads, especially the daughters. And there's no lovely fabric in summer colors! There aren't even buttons for the policemen's tunics!"

"And no money to change the situation," Mrs. Wilkinson added. "Worse comes to worst, I suppose everyone but the pirates and policemen could just wear their usual Sherborn uniforms—"

"*No!*" It was a cry from the heart. A cry of *passion*. "It wouldn't be right!" I stopped. "We *deserve* pretty dresses, Mrs. Wilkinson. We've been working so hard—"

She caught my hand and pressed it. "You needn't explain all this to me, Libby. You needn't justify your desire for a pretty frock, either. I understand completely." She gave another squeeze and relinquished my hand. "And I agree. But what can we do?"

I kicked back in my chair. "You did take up the problem with Superintendent Hodder? You did ask her?"

"Not only asked. Begged. No money in the budget."

My spirits descended further. I wracked my brains. "I don't suppose . . . those rich visitors?"

"I believe I've used them up with the blackboard

and reams of paper and other stationery supplies we're working with. Not to mention that baton and metronome."

I sank back into gloom.

"*Psst*, Libby!"

Second-Story Sal caught me on my way in to lunch. She pulled me out of sight around the nearest corner.

"What is it, Sal?"

"No luck with the costumes yet?"

I shook my head.

"Thought not. Rosie and me been worrying about it also. We been thinking, too."

"Yes?"

"You know how this place has got all those tunnels right under the building?"

"Sort of. I never really got to explore them, except for that one storage room that's filled with ancient furniture—"

"I saw a little more back when I was sent to solitary for that food fight, remember?"

"How could I forget the food fight?"

Sal snickered. "Anyhow, it gave me an idea."

I peeked around the corner. "Almost everyone's

already inside. We'd better join them before Big Bertha starts counting."

"In a minute. Listen. Tomorrow's Sunday. We've got that free period after chapel and lunch. When they let us outside to wander around for the afternoon. Meet me and Rosie. It's time for a little reconnoitering of the dungeons."

The tiniest hint of possibilities was born within my breast. "You don't suppose there'd be anything of value?"

"Sherborn's been in business for forty years, Libby. What happens to all our private things they steal from us when we get sent here? Think about it."

I thought about it. On the one hand, my pulse was already pounding—on the other, my brain was chanting *trouble, trouble, trouble* in perfect time with my pulse. Libby Dodge, human metronome. "But if we get caught in theft—"

"Theft? Of our own stuff?" Sal clapped me on the back. "That's why you're invited. For *bona fides*. The mission's gotta be legit with Wilkinson's assistant along."

I fought off my sheer lust for a lovely costume and dug in my heels. "Maybe we ought to ask Mrs. Wilkinson—"

"Come on, Libby. It's *her* we mean to surprise! She's been so wore out lately, we thought to take the weight of the costumes off her back." Sal grinned and cracked her knuckles. "Besides, Rosie and me been out of practice too long. It's time to sharpen up our skills. Even if it ain't proper breaking and entering, it'll still be fun."

CHAPTER 10

With a lump of anxiety in my stomach, Sunday lunch seemed never-ending. It was usually the fanciest meal of the week. When we were good, that meant that, instead of stew, there might be chicken. Yet what the kitchen chose to do with that chicken was often a criminal act in itself. Today it was served in the form of a watery soup with limp noodles, followed by platters of soggy carrots and onions and the stringy remains of the birds. It made me feel sorry for the creatures who'd been sentenced to execution for such results. I swirled the broth, then set my spoon aside. Sunday night's supper was always brown bread and beans. For some reason Mary and her kitchen staff did seem to have a feeling for Boston baked beans. I'd save my appetite for the evening.

Seated on my left as usual, Ma poked me. "You feelin' poorly, Libby?"

"Just not hungry, Ma."

She gave me a shrewd look. "Then pass over the bowl. Waste not, want not."

I watched Ma pick up my bowl and guzzle its contents with relish. She might complain about the quality of the prison food, but that didn't keep the woman from consuming it in quantity. Ma McCreary did everything with relish. What a pity all that life and energy would be wasted forever in Sherborn.

"Whatcha starin' at then, girl?"

"Nothing, Ma." Now I had to figure out how to slip away from my best friend to do the deed with Sal and Rosie.

I left Ma to her third helping of chicken and escaped at last into a brilliant late-June afternoon. Even its glory couldn't cure my growing nausea. I knew the symptoms too well. They'd come before every job I'd ever done. Cramps and nausea wracking my body. Doubts filling my brain. Quintus reminding me of my debts.

I took a deep breath. Think of my potatoes growing in the garden. Think of lying on the grass soaking up the sun. Don't think about disappearing into the gloom of the prison's bowels. It was madness to give up the freedom of such a summer day for Second-Story Sal's crazy scheme. Even for the most fantastic gown ever seen upon the stage . . . and me within it, giving Mabel the kind of verve, the kind of passion that could only come from a beauty in full bloom, gracefully at ease with herself and her trappings. The vision began shutting out the sunshine. I stamped temptation away. *I didn't have to do it—*

"Libby! Hold on!"

Sal and Rosie sidled up to me. They were trying to be nonchalant, but they weren't the best actresses in the world.

Sal winked hugely. "Ready, Libby?"

My resolve was weakening by the instant. "I don't think you two really need me—"

"Cold feet ain't in the picture." Kid-Glove Rosie hauled me back in the direction of the building. "We only got a few hours. Have to make the most of them."

Trapped between the two, I faced the dark stone fortress. It always ended this way. Libby Dodge the Wonder Girl—the Only Living Female with the Spine of a Worm! Yet today *was* different from the other times. I *was* doing this job for Mrs. Wilkinson. For the show. For Gilbert and Sullivan.

For *Mabel*. I tried another cleansing breath, felt the cramps ease up, then spotted Ma. She was strolling from the building—chattering head-to-head with Gladys!

When they caught sight of us, Gladys did her usual sniff and wafted off in the opposite direction. Good riddance. Unfortunately, Ma McCreary made a beeline straight at us.

"Crank up yer jaw, Libby." She paused for a healthy belch. "Ah, that's better. . . . Now, Gladys and me, we was only discussin' that first bit of dialogue we shares. You know, where me and the Major-General mixes up the words *orphan* and *orften*."

"You mean *often*."

"That's what I said, *orften*."

"Ma, it's pronounced *off-ten*."

"That's what Gladys kept on sayin', and I says she ain't got no right to go correctin' my speech just 'cause I'm not no blue-blood Yankee—" Ma stopped suddenly to peer suspiciously at the three of us. "What you all up to, then? You ain't headin' back inside on such a glorious day!"

"We, uh—"

"Have some Gilbert and Sullivan business to

attend to," Second-Story Sal muttered.

"Private business," Rosie added.

Ma did that thing with her hands on her hips. "It's mischief you're up to! I won't have my girl drug into one of your messes!"

"Ma," I pleaded. "Don't shout so. We're trying to be *discreet*."

Ma grabbed my arm and hung on like a leech. "About what?" she demanded.

Sal pulled us all into the cover of a grove of mulberries left over from some long-ago silkmaking scheme. "All right, since you had to butt in, it's the tunnels underneath the prison we're planning on exploring—"

"In search of fine cloth for the costumes!" Rosie finished.

Ma stared at them both, then began jamming ripe mulberries down her gullet. "How in tarnation you figure on finding *anything* fine down in them dungeons?" She swallowed and reached to a sheltering branch for another fistful. "And you, Libby girl," Ma shook a free finger at me. "Barely well, and intendin' to muck through that filth. You'll get yourself all infected again!"

Here was my excuse, my way out, but that wormlike spine of mine stiffened with unexpected stubbornness, for all the wrong reasons. "Really, Ma—"

Second-Story Sal sighed long and loud. "Damnation, Belle McCreary, it's clear what you're up to. Have it your way like usual. Just come along with us and protect your girl if you must."

Ma swiped mulberry juice from her mouth and beamed. That's what she'd wanted all along. To be a member of the expedition. "Well, since you puts it that-a-ways—"

Sal shook her frizzy head and began squishing through the fallen bounty of berries. At the edge of the grove she held us back while reconnoitering the fifty feet of enemy territory between us and the door.

"All clear!" she whispered, then dramatically duck and wove her way back to the prison. Rosie and Ma played along with her game. I rubbed my stomach and straightened my spine.

"*For Mabel!*" I cried, and pursued as if off to the crusades.

*   *   *

We managed to slip inside unseen. Small wonder. Every rational woman in Sherborn was lolling about in the sunshine as far from the fortress as possible. Next we were safely behind the heavy door leading down. Sal paused atop the stone stairs.

"Clean as a whistle. Ain't nobody gonna follow our trail." She reached for something. "Here we go. I managed to cop a few lanterns."

"You steal some matches to go with them things, too?" Ma asked.

I nudged her. "Don't insult Sal, Ma. This was her idea. And it could be a good one, too. It's our last chance for saving the costumes!"

Ma grumbled, but as Sal scratched a match on the wall to light the lanterns, we all lit up along with them. The blackness before us took on mysterious shapes. Our enthusiasm returned as the mission became an adventure. We tiptoed down the worn steps in a line. At the bottom was the storeroom where I'd been allowed to forage for my desk and chair once I'd been promoted to the lowest rung of Sherborn's merit system. I paused hopefully.

"You know there's nothing in there but old broken furniture." Second-Story Sal took command

and moved us forward. "Now, straight ahead here on the left, for them who haven't had the privilege, we got the real dungeons."

She pointed at a long row of iron bars. I edged up and tried to peer between them to see what was beyond.

This time it was Rosie who pulled me away. "You don't want to know what solitary looks like, Libby." The crow's feet at the corners of her eyes tightened. "Believe me."

Then we were deeper into the darkness, wandering through long, cavelike tunnels. They made me shiver. "It really is like some ancient castle," I whispered. "Just like where they imprisoned the Count of Monte Cristo for years and years."

"Never heard of him," Ma said.

"It's a story, Ma. Edmond Dantès was imprisoned falsely, and had to scratch his way to freedom and revenge, only by that time he was nearly an old man, with a long beard, and—"

"Hah!" Second-Story Sal turned a corner and halted. We scurried up to her. She'd stopped before a big wooden door with a huge, rusty iron padlock dangling from it.

"Told you there was something hidden down here."

"Treasure!" Rosie yelped.

"Remains to be seen," Ma griped. She tugged at me as I tried to get closer. "You steer clear, Libby. Just look at that rust. Could be more of them lockjaw germs on that thing."

Try as I might to be brave and adventurous, Ma just wasn't going to allow it. I broke away rebelliously. "Want me to hold your lantern, Sal, so you can inspect it?"

"Fat lot of good that'll do." Ma must've gotten up on the wrong side of the bed this morning, and the results were still with her. Even after all that chicken. "Ain't nobody gettin' through that lock without a file or bolt cutter."

Second-Story Sal smiled. "Care to place a bet on that, Belle McCreary? A good solid bet, like your supper for the next week or two?"

Ma shrugged. "I ain't a bettin' woman. Get on with it, then."

Sal got on with it. She handed me the lantern, then fished a hairpin from her head and hunkered over the padlock, softly singing the words to her first solo as the Pirate King's Lieutenant:

"For to-day our pirate 'prentice
Rises from indentures freed;
Strong his arm, and keen his scent is
He's a pirate now indeed!"

Before she had the opportunity to move on to the second verse, there was a scratchy click, a metallic groan, and Sal rose upright to tug the hasp open.

"You owe me some suppers, Belle."

"Never placed the bet, Sal, and you knows it."

Sal grinned. "Don't matter. Second-Story Sal still has the touch."

"I'll give you that, Sal. I will indeed." Ma grinned back, her humor restored at last. Rosie pulled at the door, and we all pushed to get inside.

I raised the lantern and stopped dead. "We found the trunk room!" I cried.

Before us were trunks—hundreds of trunks—piled helter-skelter, most covered with years of dust and cobwebs. I poked at an extravagant web design that had been labored over long and hard. "How could spiders get down here? How could they *live* down here?"

"Must be the extras from solitary," Sal answered.

Ma caught my blanch. "Don't matter, Libby. You'll never be seeing solitary anyhow." She rubbed her hands. "Now what're we waitin' on? Let's have at some of this here treasure!"

I directed the lantern to the closest pile, the cleanest one. Setting the lamp to rest nearby, I tentatively freed the clasp of the topmost trunk and pushed open the lid.

"*Gad!*"

"What is it, Libby?"

Sal, Rosie, and Ma were jostling each other to get near enough to see what I did. Instead of giving way, I bent into the trunk and came forth with—

"It's my silk straw hat! With its wreath of daisies!" I gave the beloved object a shake—no nesting spiders—and set it jauntily on my head. "You have no idea how I've longed for this hat! Dreamed of it!"

"It's a pert enough topper," Ma agreed, "but what's that piece of paper stuck to the brim?"

I pulled off the hat to inspect the pinned label. "It's got my name on it! 'Property of Libby Dodge.' Does that mean they were intending to give it back to me?"

"Hard to say. Don't look like the authorities been too prompt about returning anything down here." Ma brushed the remains of a cobweb from her face.

"What else we got in there? Any dresses? Anything Agnes and her crew can tear apart and put back together again?"

I dove back inside to emerge with the very outfit I'd arrived in at Sherborn. It was a tasteful afternoon suit, with the flared skirt that was the very latest in fashion. At least it had been, some months back. I fingered the softness of the pale blue wool and crocheted buttons, longing more than anything to tear off my ugly uniform and surround my body with its caress.

Sal caught my hunger. "It's wool, Libby. Wrong season for today. You'd roast. Too heavy for the play, too. What else we got?"

I set my lovely suit back within the trunk and we moved on to other trunks, other seasons.

Much later—how much later none of us noticed—we had the contents of dozens of trunks strewn around the room. We'd been hauling out dresses, studying the cloth for potential use, filling our apron pockets with brass and gold-colored buttons that could be used for the policemen's tunics. We were having a very good time. It was Ma who came to her senses first with a little jolt.

"Me stomach alarm just set off."

"So what?" Sal asked. She'd found some colored scarves and had them rakishly wrapped around her head, pirate-fashion.

"*So what* is that me stomach works like a clock. When it starts to growling, I know it's time for the next meal." She stopped to let us digest the dimensions of her information.

"Supper?" I squeaked.

"Supper."

"Aw, hell," Rosie said. She'd just found a cape with the most luscious red satin lining and was parading in it.

"What'll we do?" I asked. "How will we get back without anyone noticing?"

"Let 'em notice!" Sal exclaimed. "We got Mrs. Wilkinson's present just like we set out for. With such loot as this, we'll be the heroines of the day!"

We each grabbed as much of the clothing as we could carry and scurried through the darkness. Even though our arms began to sag, our spirits stayed high all the way through the tunnels, past the dungeons, and up the final flight of stone steps. Then Sal blew out the lanterns, carefully set them down, and opened the door to the upper world.

"Oh!" I gasped.

Hovering there like vultures waiting for the kill was the rest of Sherborn. At least, Superintendent Hodder—along with Big Bertha and her cohorts. Behind them smirked Gladys.

"There! I told you so! They left a trail of squashed mulberries clear to the basement door." Gladys tossed her head in triumph.

My eyes darted from Judas to the superintendent.

"Libby Dodge," she intoned. "Mrs. McCreary. Sal and Rosie. Would you care to explain yourselves?"

Mrs. Wilkinson dashed up as our booty fell to the floor.

"The *Pirates of Penzance*—" I tried.

"Needed costumes," Ma continued.

"We found them!" Sal exulted.

"Without permission," Mrs. Hodder noted. "By stealth and intrigue." She turned to Bertha. "Since they seem so fond of the place, you may escort them back downstairs, Matron. To solitary this time. Two full weeks for each of them."

"Please, Mrs. Hodder," Mrs. Wilkinson pleaded.

"Libby and Mrs. McCreary and Sal and Rosie are the leading players in our production! They've invested their hearts and souls in it! Their intentions were honorable. Their only crime was to use a little initiative—"

"But no common sense. Permission could have been requested through legitimate means," the superintendent stated flatly.

Mrs. Wilkinson tried once more. "But these women made no effort to hide what they found. They returned with these dresses for the good of all. For the good of Sherborn!"

Mrs. Hodder blinked. "Fair enough. Mercy shall be shown. *One* week in solitary detention. Get on with it, Matron."

"*Mulberries!*" Ma snorted.

She grabbed my arm and there was only time to cast a quick, despairing look at Mrs. Wilkinson before returning to the lower depths.

CHAPTER 11

"**B**een waiting a long time for your comeuppance." Bertha leered with grim satisfaction as she shoved me through the gate in the outer bars. "Enjoy your new crib, princess."

She waved her lantern toward the cell awaiting me. There was only a moment to take in the dimensions of the room: small. Very small. As for its contents, they consisted in entirety of a wooden shelf jutting from the windowless stone wall, a jug of water, and a chamber pot.

"What about a blanket?" I tried.

Too late. The heavy door was slamming shut. I barely caught Ma's cry from beyond.

"Buck up, Libby girl. You can do it! You—"

Silence. Complete and total darkness. That's what I was left with. I flung out my arms for balance, took a tentative step forward, and tripped on the chamber pot. That clever move flung me face-first into the bed shelf. I sprawled in that awkward position a few moments, panicking.

Pull yourself together, Libby Dodge. Ma can't help you now. Nobody can. You're on your own again.

I forced a few deep breaths, then clambered atop the shelf and felt for my forehead. It would soon be sporting a nasty bruise. Little matter. There'd be no one to see it.

Tucking my legs beneath me, I wrapped my arms around my body. Seven days and seven nights in this hellhole. Twenty-four hours a day times seven. I did the multiplication in my head. One hundred and sixty-eight hours. Each filled with sixty minutes. Gilbert and Sullivan had some apologizing to do. My body began to rock on the wooden shelf. Back and forth, back and forth. Just like Ruby.

A creak in the direction of the door brought me to my senses some time later. I rubbed my eyes and squinted through the blackness, trying to find something, any-thing, to cast light on my situation. I was rewarded by a sliver of lamplight peeking through the bottom of the door. . . . The bottom of the door? The square of light increased as a tiny door set within the larger one squeaked open. I pounced at it in time to watch a tin plate being nudged through the opening, followed by a sloshing tin cup.

"Yer supper," a faint voice notified me.

I snatched at the plate and cup as the opening latched shut once more. My finger dove into the lukewarm liquid. So this is what it was like to be blind. I shook the finger, then managed to grasp the handle and raise the cup to my lips. Coffee. Unsweetened black coffee. Very gingerly this time, I made my way across the cell—all of two steps—and settled myself on the bed. After swallowing another sip of the harsh brew, I felt for the plate. Boston baked beans suddenly swam through my head. Boston baked beans thick with molasses and layered with tender chunks of pork. What my hand met was bread. Not moist, nutty, buttered brown bread, either. Hard, dry bread. Did the kitchen save its week-old leftovers for this very purpose? I would have to have a chat with Mary about this when I got out. If I got out.

As I'd foolishly skipped lunch, my stomach felt emptier than it ever had in my recent life. I broke off a chunk of the bread and dunked it in the coffee. If I was really, really careful I might be able to stretch this meal into at least a half hour. That would be thirty minutes spent of my solitary confinement. Thirty minutes I wouldn't have to live through again.

Night. It must be night. Supper was finished. I curled up on the bench and tried to analyze where Ma and Sal and Rosie and I had gone wrong.

Permission, Superintendent Hodder had wanted. Why hadn't we asked her for permission? That was clear enough. The idea had never crossed our minds. Second-Story Sal—well, I wouldn't expect it to have occurred to her. Half of the purpose of the expedition for Sal had been the lark of being back in business again. Kid-Glove Rosie probably came under the same category. Ma? I considered. Well, Ma had come along for the ride. With her status she wouldn't be likely to ask permission for anything. Being stuck in Sherborn for the remainder of her natural life the way she was, Ma McCreary was hardly the woman to care about following the rules. What more could they do to punish her, after all? A stay in solitary now and again? Solitary wasn't about to stop Ma.

I uncurled long enough to transfer my empty plate and cup to the floor, then spread out full length on the shelf. That was a mistake. The boards of my bed were splintery. It was chilly down here, too—a damp, musty sort of chill that went straight for the marrow of my bones. I curled up in a tight ball again to continue my examination of the situation.

Left to consider were my own motives in the aborted operation. Why hadn't it occurred to *me* to request permission from the superintendent? *Trouble* had been my first reaction to the mission, hadn't it? And I *had* halfheartedly suggested trying for Mrs. Wilkinson's approval. Sal had talked me out of that much too easily. . . . No, my hunger for a lovely gown had done the real talking. My hunger for a little elegance in a gray place. I suppose it was hard to starve the *prima donna* out of me.

My mind strayed back to that earlier conversation with Mrs. Hodder. The one in which she'd told me to think, to use some *common sense*. What if . . .

There were too many *what-ifs* in my life already. What if I had gone to Mrs. Hodder for permission? What if I hadn't made a debacle of that last job and never ended up in Sherborn? What if I hadn't been orphaned at a tender age, leaving me to the questionable care and guidance of Dr. Quintus Wylie Gill? Definitely too many *what-ifs*. I closed my eyes, though it was hardly necessary, and drifted into an uncomfortable sleep.

The jiggling of that little door woke me with a start. Unfortunately, I was too woozy to scramble to the opposite side of the room before the sliver of light disappeared once more. But anticipation brought me to alertness quickly enough. I almost jumped from my perch, then forced myself to move with caution. As bad as the dungeon coffee was, its warmth would be welcome. I edged off the bed, slipped to my knees, and groped across the remaining two feet of rough stone flooring until my fingers came up against the expected breakfast: more stale bread and lukewarm coffee.

Several thoughts brightened the discovery. First, I now knew that breakfast and supper would be served, probably on a regular basis. The question of lunch could be left to the future. Secondly, I realized I had actually survived my first night in solitary. That meant half a day of the sentence was over, leaving but six and a half more. I grinned between sips of the coffee. A cinch!

After breakfast I busied myself with little housekeeping tasks. I carefully removed the pins from my hair, let it fall past my shoulders, then painstakingly wove it into a long plait. That would keep it neater for the duration. Next, I splashed my face with water from the jug, and performed my other ablutions. I cautiously moved all the empty plates and cups to the floor-level hatch, shoved the chamber pot directly to the front, and fervently hoped my keeper would take the hint and remove them all.

Then I paced off the length and width of the room. It came to a neat six-foot square. I tried running my hands along the stones in search of any potential cracks or crevices like those Alexandre Dumas's hero had found in *The Count of Monte Cristo*. I guess I had some silly romantic notion that it could be possible to communicate with Ma or the others through the solid granite walls—or even to escape. The summer world above these dungeons was more enticing than it ever had been. All that sunshine being wasted without me to see it!

But escape only happened in novels. In the real universe, I quickly gave up on the effort when my fingers dislodged a tiny creature that scuttled away. A spider? No. This one had a hard shell. I shivered. More likely a cockroach. I sat myself down on the rough wooden shelf which for daytime purposes I now thought of as my sofa. I had accomplished absolutely everything I could think of to accomplish. I folded my hands. The next twelve hours of the day spread out before me.

Luncheon was not served in the Sherborn dungeons. It was evening before my carefully placed tin and crockery—joined by then with the empty water jug—were all removed and replaced. In the interim I'd learned a few things:

> A. Gilbert and Sullivan cannot be sung for twelve solid hours at a time—and Handel's "Hallelujah Chorus" was inappropriate to both the circumstances and the milieu.

> B. There weren't nearly enough spiders in Sherborn's dungeons to cope with its army of cockroaches.

I ate my second supper of stale bread before the roaches attacked for their share, and allowed myself to curl up on my bed. Mentally I scratched off one complete day. The first twenty-four hours. Only six more days to survive in solitary confinement.

I will not let the darkness madden me. I will not scream into the silence. I will be strong.

After breakfast of the second day my will faltered. I'd been fighting with every ounce of strength in my body. The constant darkness was too much. Libby Dodge, Wonder Girl, lost the battle again.

The past took over.

The gems arrived first, probably because of the brass buttons I'd rediscovered in my apron pocket. I fingered the buttons, then retrieved them to stack in little piles on the wooden planks next to me. They became something else.

Gems were the earliest playthings I could remember. Little piles of hard, sparkling colors to sort through, to hold before a window so rays of sunlight could make rainbows to set me laughing. Learning words and rhymes through them:

Red is for ruby, so rare and so bright.
Green is for emerald that catches the light.
Blue is for sapphire, the ladies' delight.

The long-forgotten chant on my lips brought Papa back. Tears came with the memory. He'd been tall, thin, hollow-chested; a serious man with a thick shock of wavy black hair. A lapidary and jeweler. How could it be surprising then, that one of my first toys was a loupe? There would be no dolls for his precious, only child, bereft of her mother since infancy. There would be something better—those mounds of jewels spread upon soft black velvet.

I adored Papa in return. We were inseparable. Neither could bear to be parted when it came time for school, so Papa taught me instead, right there in the shop below our rooms. Addition and subtraction were easy when dealing with heaps of diamonds or pearls. His library of lore on curious and precious stones was more fascinating reading than any fairy tale. I was already learning the intricacies of facets, and the difference between *brilliant* cuts versus *marquise* or *radiant* or *trillion*, when consumption took him from me.

Papa taught me to the bitter end, his soft, gentle

voice pausing only long enough to cough ruby-red blood into immaculate linen handkerchiefs. I knew how to tell if a stone was symmetrically balanced; if there were cracks or scratches on a stone's table; and certainly what a carat was. Unfortunately, I knew little else. I was seven.

Enter my guardian, my father's excellent customer and friend: Dr. Quintus Wylie Gill—a small, dapper man complete with goatee, pince-nez, and expensive tastes. He was a prominent physician who kept a private Boston sanitarium for wealthy women with "reflex nervous trouble which renders them at times unaccountable for their actions." Quintus snatched my inheritance, slung me in an orphanage, then promptly forgot about me.

Quintus.

I fumbled in my apron pocket for a handkerchief to swab at my damp face. That was the last time I'd truly cried. In the orphanage. Every night for that first lonely year I'd lie in my tiny cot in a long row of other cots, crying myself to sleep. One morning I woke up with words in my head: *You're on your own, Libby Dodge. Nobody cares about you anymore. No one ever will, here in this place. Save your tears and learn to be strong.*

I tried to teach myself to be strong. I might even have been making progress. I'd certainly learned to lock away my emotions while scrubbing miles of floors, and peeling mountains of potatoes. It was only when I was on duty with the foundlings—changing diapers and feeding bottles—that I let my defenses down. The poor little souls had tougher lives ahead of them than I ever would. At least I'd known a loving parent. Whenever one of them died—despite all the lullabies sung, all the hugs and kisses I could lavish on them—I fell apart. Over and over again.

Drained by images of my lost foundlings, I stretched out on the bench, splinters or no. I stared straight up into the blackness that was no longer black. The lowering ceiling over my head that I could feel, if not see, became a screen from one of the movie houses on Washington Street. I'd ducked into them now and again when there wasn't a new play to divert me. With the same mannered acting, a melodrama projected itself above me—an unseen piano player in the orchestra banging out accompaniment. The plot was simple: a story about unwanted babies. Rows of cribs lined a nursery. I was the ten-year-old star—pitiful in worn and patched sackcloth—mothering as best I could. Enter the satin-draped villain: Gladys. Black-and-white changed to hand-tinted color. But only the blankets were tinted. Pink and blue.

"*Stop the show!*" I screamed. "*Stop it!*"

The projectionist cut the light.

I wound myself like a contortionist around the pain in my gut as Quintus reappeared.

A series of his clients had presented Dr. Gill with the most brilliant of scams imaginable. Quintus came to call it "department-store hysteria," or "kleptomania," in his learned papers.

He testified in court for one woman after another who'd been arrested for stealing the pretty trinkets lying so readily at hand on the counters of Filene's and every other high-class department store in Boston. Quintus's defense was always the same: Mrs. Filbrick or Madame Boothman *never* intended to steal. Blame their unconscious minds. They'd been hypnotised by the incredible goods displayed behind the plate-glass windows lining the shopping streets. Hypnotised by the beautiful objects lying in wait on counters in the stores' interiors. Under the umbrella of Dr. Gill's Freudian mumbo jumbo, his ladies always got off scot-free to return home to their mansions and husbands—only slightly chastened.

Quintus Wylie Gill proved to have a more fertile unconscious than any of his women. I was eleven and beginning to mature early when he plucked me from the orphanage. He pressed beautiful clothing upon me and reminded me of my interest in precious objects. Then he sent me out chained to an invisible tether to become the classic kleptomaniac. On purpose.

As I appeared well bred and was well dressed, the floorwalkers and security guards always overlooked me. I trod and pilfered where Sal and Rosie never could have gone. And returned the goods to Quintus Wylie Gill. Of course I did. I had no choice. Because Quintus held the perfect blackmail over my head: *my mother.*

I thought Mama was dead. Papa had always told me she was in heaven. Three days after I'd been *rescued* from the orphanage I learned differently. Quintus Wylie Gill took me out of the sackcloth I'd spent the last four years in and dressed me up like a doll. He stuffed me with sweets till I thought *I'd* gone to heaven. When my defenses were down, when he'd almost convinced me I was still the innocent seven-year-old he'd abandoned to the orphanage, he took the hand I rashly placed in his and led me down one of his sanitarium corridors. Removing a key from his pocket, he opened a door. He pointed to a wretch within.

"There you see the unfortunate results of a trolley-car accident, my dear child."

The tone of that *my dear child* didn't sound right. Feel right. I pulled my hand from his. "Who is this poor creature?"

"Quite unresponsive for more than ten years," he continued, "since you were an infant, in fact—"

Why was he bringing me into his story? My stomach began to ache.

"Unresponsive, save for occasional moments of violent madness. Hence the charming accommodations." Dr. Quintus Wylie Gill paused to beam upon me. "Do say hello to your mother, Libby Dodge."

"It can't be! My mama's in heaven with the angels!"

My stomach felt worse. Felt so bad that I lurched

past the doctor and threw up all that cake and candy on the sparkling floor of the corridor. My *mother*. In that room. Somehow I believed. I wiped my mouth with one of my fancy new lace handkerchiefs, shoved it back in my pocket, and crossed the threshold of the terrible room. She was trussed up in a straitjacket and propped against a padded wall. The room held nothing else save a cot. I inched closer.

"Mama? Mama. It's me, Libby."

Mama's eyes were open, but they saw nothing, held nothing. Those eyes would never change. I know. I studied them every day for five years.

"So now you understand, my dear child."

I walked out of the padded cell and kicked Quintus Wylie Gill on the shins. Hard.

"I'm *not* your dear child."

Quintus nursed his leg. "Understood. But *you* must understand something, as well," he snarled. "Your father left me his estate to look after your mother in perpetuity, as it were. There was hardly enough for *perpetuity*. Now it's your turn. You are legally my ward, and you will work to support your sweet mama's upkeep."

"How?" I growled. I could be surly, too.

"I will teach you how. I will civilize you in the process. I expect our relationship to be long and beneficial."

"Who for?"

"For me, of course. And your mother. For you, too—if you learn to play the game."

Quintus shut the door and turned the key. He presented it to me. "A gift. So you may remember—and learn your responsibilities."

I learned my responsibilities. Mama's mind may have been in heaven with the angels, but her body remained in Dr. Quintus Wylie Gill's padded cell. And her eyes never changed. Not during the long five years I studied them.

A rattling hatch made the agony of those vacant eyes disappear. Suppertime? Or was it breakfast? Of which day? My insides were still cramped from hunger—or remembrance. Maybe both. I stretched from my rigid coil and rose. As I automatically pressed creases from my uniform, unseen vermin scrabbled to the floor. I'd known worse horrors. I staggered across the cell for my stale bread.

The ache in my stomach could not be cured with bread or coffee or water. Worse was the ache in my very soul. Try as I might to banish him, Quintus kept returning. Quintus and his blackmail.

Dr. Gill was a very fiend for innovations upon his original demands. The last year had been the worst. That's when he raised the ante. Those pince-nez couldn't hide the sly deviousness in his eyes when I was released from my room one evening, elegantly dressed, to join him for dinner.

I nodded and sat. Waited for the soup to be served. When the servant disappeared, Quintus picked up his spoon.

"Do try the vichyssoise. It looks excellent this evening."

It wasn't potato-and-leek soup he was thinking about. I'd grown to know him too well. I allowed my cold soup to sit there, waiting. It came.

"You do look lovely this evening, my dear Libby. The new couturier I recommended is a master of color and line." He delicately spooned and swallowed his soup. "In fact—"

I steeled myself within the rigidity of my corset.

"In fact, I do believe you've matured sufficiently to graduate."

"To what?" The words slipped out despite my best intentions.

"Why, to more lucrative establishments, of course. Fine jewelry stores."

Quintus's silent servant removed my untouched soup and replaced it with the fish course. Trout meunière. I stared at it. A milky eye stared back. My stomach rebelled.

"It's what you've been planning all along, isn't it?"

"How acute of you. Why waste your one precocious skill, after all? Not everyone has an innate feeling for gems. Not everyone can choose the one flawless diamond from among a hundred, the single perfect pearl amidst a dozen strings."

Unseen hands filled my wine glass. I grasped for it and drank.

"That's an especially fine Bordeaux, Libby. Please show it some consideration."

I groped for my water jug. Tipped it to my lips. Empty. My mouth was dry, incredibly dry. How long since I'd remembered to shove the jug by the little door for refilling? No matter. I tossed it into the void. Its explosion lit the next memory.

My successes multiplied, yet they only made Quintus pensive. One evening over his after-dinner cigar he floated a new idea.

"Perhaps we ought to have a contingency plan for your protection, Libby dear."

"In case I'm collared one of these days?"

He frowned. "Colloquialisms are so lower class."

I ignored the jibe. "Never tell me you're becoming concerned about my well-being!"

He blew a ring of smoke and watched it rise toward the chandelier above us. "More, I'll admit, about my bank account. And your mother's contin-ued upkeep, of course."

"I've already paid her debt a thousand times over. When will you release me?"

"*Tsk.* I supposed you to be more clever than that. You'll *never* finish paying her debt—not to mention yours."

"*Mine!*"

Quintus took his time nudging ashes from his cigar. "All the preparations for your role. Expensive clothing. The odd tutor over the years: French, deportment . . . Shall I continue?"

Snared. What I'd begun to suspect was true. He'd never set me free. "What did you have in mind?"

"A little something known in the legal world as *feme covert*. As my wife, you'd have a certain defense—"

I flung the napkin I'd been twisting onto the table and rose. "Rather than marry you, Quintus, I'd spend my life behind bars—in a *legitimate* prison. Not this sanitarium of yours."

He laughed. "How droll. You'll concede. You always do."

I didn't. I made a final pilgrimage to my mother. I explained my dilemma to her. I begged forgiveness. She heard nothing. Neither did she feel the last kiss I gave her. After that, it was easy to slip during my next job. Easy to allow myself to be collared.

When Quintus used his "reflex nervous trouble" defense on the court, it didn't work. Even my taking the stand to vigorously defend my "physical inability" to resist the lure of the gems I'd almost purloined didn't help. My pleas were never *that* vigorous, of course. Downcast eyes and maidenly innocence were part of the role. Quintus had schooled me, hadn't he? Besides, there wasn't much point in receiving an impossible sentence. I knew the length I needed: just long enough to escape from the clutches of Dr. Quintus Wylie Gill; just long enough to break from my unconscionable pattern of thievery. Just long enough to learn what it was like to be in charge of myself, to learn how to make my own decisions. As Mrs. Hodder would put it, to learn how to *think*.

It was during my trial that Quintus officially aged me a year to seventeen—for his own protection. No need for him to be drawn into a morals charge involving a minor.

None of it worked this time—because my "kleptomania" had nearly netted a haul of more than five thousand dollars in diamonds and pearls. Grand larceny was a step up from Filene's.

I'd unconsciously unplaited and replaited my hair who knows how many times. I only noticed when I found the tattered length in my hands once more. I gave it rough tug. That didn't banish Quintus, but it did return me to reality. In reality, I was sprawled on the dank floor of an isolation cell in the Sherborn Prison for Women. It wasn't as elegant as my locked room in Quintus's sanitarium. It held none of the Dumas and Dickens novels with which I'd wiled away the hours between jobs. Despite everything, it felt *clean*. I smiled into the blackness. It was a good beginning, after all.

No more tears. I returned the buttons to my apron pocket and began singing Gilbert and Sullivan once more. I made my own peace with my poor mother. I made my peace with my conscience. I'd never have to lay eyes upon Dr. Quintus Wylie Gill again. In my euphoria—probably induced by starvation as much as soul-searching—only one thought kept me from embracing the very stone walls imprisoning me.

What next?

What would happen after my release from Sherborn? What could the future hold for an orphan ex-convict whose only talent was a knowledge of extravagant gems? What kind of a future waited for a young woman whose crime had been genteel larceny? My euphoric high plunged to the depths of despair.

The orphanage. The sanitarium. Sherborn.

Would I ever escape my life history of incarceration?

The evening of the seventh day arrived.

CHAPTER **12**

There was brown bread and Boston baked beans for supper. I didn't get to eat them in the dining hall, though. I didn't get to eat beans at all. Mrs. Wilkinson was waiting at the top of the stone steps when Ma and Sal and Rosie and I staggered out the door. Dr. Colbrook was, too. They took one look at the four of us and hustled us straight to the infirmary.

Besides all those neat white beds, the infirmary boasted something else: bathtubs. Not the long line of open shower stalls that lurked, darkly dripping, at the end of each dormitory wing, but real, genuine, porcelain-lined bathtubs with claw feet and hot water fed from the infirmary's very own water boiler. My spirits rose like one of Filene's escalators. Fears for my future outside Sherborn's walls dissolved. From this moment I'd try to make the best of each day, one at a time.

The private bathtub was an excellent beginning—filled with my very own fresh, clean hot water. But before I could enjoy it, Ma had to be peeled from me. She refused to let go till she laid eyes on her own waiting tub. Now she and the others were oohing and aahing and splashing behind their separate curtains, while I tore off my filthy clothes and stepped into the tub. My legs felt like rubber.

"Oh. My." I sank blissfully up to my neck. "Why are we getting this special treatment?" I asked Mrs. Wilkinson, who waited outside my curtain. "Sal and Rosie and Ma and me? When Gladys got out of solitary—"

"Gladys was not trying to save the show."

"Oh." I finally noticed the bubbles. And the scented water. "Where did . . . ?"

"Hush," Mrs. Wilkinson said. "It's my private stock of bathing supplies."

"And the shampoo?" I reached for the bottle perched above the faucet. "Sal and Rosie and Ma aren't getting the bubbles and special shampoo."

"No."

"Why am I?"

Mrs. Wilkinson sighed. "My little girl had thick black hair like yours—when it's clean. And her eyes were as blue as yours, sapphire blue. . . ."

The pain in her voice destroyed the satisfaction of a mystery solved.

"If . . . if the influenza hadn't taken her from me, Jenny would have been your age. A young lady. The moment I first saw you, I knew what she would have looked like. And when you sing—"

When I finally emerged to stand dripping in a robe, there were tears in my eyes. Tears for the mother I'd never have a chance to know. Tears for the daughter the chaplain had lost. Tears I thought I'd dried forever in solitary. Grief wasn't rational. It couldn't be abandoned with my other nightmares. "Thank you, Mrs. Wilkinson."

The chaplain blew her nose and tucked the hand-kerchief up her sleeve. "Come along, Libby. Boston baked beans are too heavy for your empty stomach. I've some broth waiting for you. Good broth."

Ma and the others had the chance to sleep in the infir-mary that night, but decided they'd rather get back to their own cells. I stayed. Dr. Colbrook carefully inspected me and declared me properly deloused. Then she anointed me with salves and unguents against the predations of the dungeon's insect population.

"You'll survive the emaciation and the bites. At least the rats left you alone," she finally declared.

"*Rats?*"

Lena Colbrook finished her ministrations. "Apparently they found Mrs. McCreary tasty. She managed to stomp two. Brought their skins out in her apron pockets as proof."

"Only the skins?" I asked. "What about the rest?"

"She said she'd 'et them.'" Dr. Colbrook shook her head. "An amazing woman."

Ma's latest exploits left me speechless. I drank my broth, burrowed gratefully beneath clean white sheets, and proceeded to sleep for the next twenty-four hours.

I woke in time for Hallelujah Hour. Feeling weak as a kitten, I once more negotiated the seeming miles between the infirmary and the assembly room. By the time I arrived the rehearsal was well under way, so I tucked myself into a corner and gave it my full attention.

Amazing things had been happening in my absence. Progress, real progress had taken place. Mrs. Wilkinson had her own theory about how to go about putting the show together. We'd discussed this at length during one of my scribbling mornings in the library. Usually, she explained, a director worked straight through a production from first scene to last.

"But, Libby," Mrs. Wilkinson said, "the policemen don't have their entrance until the second act. Now what do you suppose those particular women are likely to do if we can't get them into the action a little earlier?"

"Riot," I promptly answered.

"Precisely. So I've decided to start working with all the choruses more or less at once, then concentrate on them alternately during our rehearsals."

It was a wise decision. But then, Mrs. Wilkinson was the wisest woman I'd ever known. So here she was tonight, working with the policemen. They really did have wonderfully funny lines to sing. It was a joy sitting there listening. Being back among the living again.

Kid-Glove Rosie, the Sergeant of Police, seemed no worse for her week in solitary as she belted out the lines meant to put heart into her men as they went off to battle the pirates. And the chorus's answering refrain was enthusiasm at its height:

"When the foeman bares his steel,
Tarantara! tarantara!
We uncomfortable feel,
Tarantara!
And we find the wisest thing,
Tarantara! tarantara!
Is to slap our chests and sing,
Tarantara!"

The long and short of it is that by the time the policemen had got down to their last "Tarantara-ra-ra-ra-ra!" I felt amazingly energized. Without even thinking, I leaped to my feet and launched into *my* solo that followed.

"Go, ye heroes, go to glory—"

It only took Mrs. Wilkinson a moment to catch on and continue the music.

"Though you die in combat gory,
Ye shall live in song and story.

Go to immortality!

Go to death, and go to slaughter;
Die, and every Cornish daughter
With her tears your grave shall water.

Go, ye heroes, go and die!"

I stopped. The music stopped. Then the applause began. And the cheers.

"Welcome back, Libby!"

"Welcome back, Rosie!"

"Ma and Sal, too!"

Agnes Cordoni burst from her seat with a needle and a lovely piece of cloth in hand. "Three cheers for our own heroes what saved the play!"

"Hip hip hooray!"

"Hip hip hooray!"

"Hip hip hoor-ay!"

Well, then we had to do an encore. Isn't that what theatre is all about?

I returned to copying the final lines the next morning. It was the dialogue that went between the songs. What a pleasure to be back in the library. I stuck around for lyrics drills and the reading lessons just before lunch, and was delighted to see that Emma and her friends were making progress too. They'd progressed, in fact, all the way to the second chapter of Genesis, and were working on verses 16 and 17:

And the LORD God commanded the man, saying, Of every tree of the garden thou mayest freely eat: But of the tree of the knowledge of good and evil, thou shalt not eat of it: for in the day that thou eatest thereof thou shalt surely die.

I watched Emma take her turn to read. She had all the easy words down pat, but stumbled over "knowledge."

"Ka-ka-ka-now—"

"All right, Emma," Dr. Colbrook interrupted. "This is a perfect example of those silent consonants I mentioned. When *k* comes before *n* you don't pronounce it. It becomes invisible."

"Why?" Emma wanted to know.

Lena Colbrook shrugged. "It's just one of those rules going back to the beginning of the English language."

"More rules!" pouted Rachel. "That's what came out of eating from that silly old tree of *knowledge*—"

"Beautifully pronounced, Rachel." Dr. Colbrook smiled.

"Knowledge of *good* and *evil*," another woman spoke up. "So when you get right down to it, Eve's to blame for our being here!"

"Why?" I butted in.

"Because she ate an apple from that tree, then went and tempted Adam to have a bite too, and they got kicked out of Eden—"

"But it's not *fair* to blame Eve for everything!" I nearly shouted. "It's not *fair* to blame women for all the wickedness in the world!" I took a deep breath to calm myself. It wasn't my place to make that point, but after my experience with Quintus, I knew better.

"Libby's right," Emma said. "I went out of my papa's house into the world an innocent. It was a *man* who put me here."

The room erupted.

"Yes! It was like leaving Eden!"

"My home wasn't never no Paradise—"

"And getting stuck bearing children in pain and sorrow. That's for the birds, too."

"Ladies, please." Dr. Colbrook didn't have a baton, but she could be quietly commanding nevertheless. "It's necessary to remember that the Garden of Eden story is an allegory—"

"What's an *allegory?*"

The doctor turned to write the word on the blackboard. She wrote it out in full, then broke it down into syllables, the way I'd been doing with some of the lyrics for the *Pirates of Penzance.*

"Al-le-go-ry. It means a story which carries a second meaning beneath the plot. The plot here is Adam and Eve being banished from Eden. When the Bible was written, people were trying to figure out how if God were as good as he was supposed to be. . . ." she paused. "Well, if that were the case, why was the world in such a sorry fix."

"You mean it was in a mess way back then, too?" Emma asked.

"Unfortunately, yes. It's likely to be more of a mess than usual very soon, too."

"Why?" I asked again.

The doctor focused on me. "Why? You haven't heard? No, you wouldn't have, Libby."

"Heard what?"

"While you were 'away,' Archduke Franz Ferdinand, the heir to the throne of Austria-Hungary, was assassinated in Sarajevo. That's a city in Central Europe. In Bosnia, in fact, part of the Balkans which have always been troubled. . . ." She sighed. "The long and short of it is that the European countries are already mobilizing for war."

"All because of knowledge of the tree of good and evil." I stared at Lena Colbrook.

She stared back. "For which women were *not* responsible." She turned to the rest of the group. "The world has always needed a scapegoat, ladies. A whipping boy. Someone on whom to blame *everything*. Unfortunately, *we* are it. It's our duty to see to it that this situation changes. In every way possible." She erased the blackboard. "Lessons are over for today."

CHAPTER 13

Europe was too far away to worry about. As July burst into heat and first harvests, Sherborn's women had only one thing on their minds: Gilbert and Sullivan.

We'd gotten to the point in our rehearsals where what we needed next was a stage. A real stage. I'd borrowed a measuring tape from Sparky's tool shed, and Ma was holding down the other end of it as we valiantly tried to imagine squeezing such a stage into the assembly room.

"It ain't no good, Libby." She flung down the tape in disgust. "I appreciate you gettin' me off of garden duty on account of how I'm the resident stage expert, aside from Mrs. Wilkinson . . . but no way in hell—" Ma gave a quick look around to make sure the chaplain wasn't within hearing distance. "No way in *hell* we gonna fit any kind of a decent stage in this here assembly room."

"Even if we blocked off the front third of the room?" I tried.

"Go ahead and block off the front third. Then figure on movin' the pianner down in front of that. Then start addin' in rows of chairs for the superintendent's honored guests." Ma waved around the room. "What you got left then, Libby?"

I frowned, picturing the congestion. "Not enough space for the rest of Sherborn to see the show. And we've *got* to have room for every last woman not on stage to be part of the audience. Everyone's involved. Everyone deserves to be part of our opening night!"

"Percisely." Ma put her hands on her hips and squeezed her eyes tightly shut. "Gotta think. Must be some other place in this here jumble of wings and buildings. . . . Hah!" Her eyes popped open. "It come to me. Just like that. The machine room!"

"The sewing-machine room? But that's stuffed with machines!"

"No, no. The *other*, spare machine room. The empty one. What nobody goes into ever."

I was already winding up the tape. "What are we waiting for? Let's take a look."

* * *

The empty machine room wasn't empty. It had the same vast space as Agnes Cordoni's headquarters and the same tall windows (filthy), but it seemed to be filled with the detritus from building Sherborn forty years back.

"Drat!" I stumbled over a pile of lumber, then rubbed at my shin and righted myself. "It's got the space all right, Ma, but it's going to take about a year to clear out all this trash."

Ma was grinning ear to ear. "Trash? I don't see no trash. What we got for ourselves here is enough wood to cobble together a stage as big as the Old Howard Theatre's!" She chortled. "All we need is Sparky and some tools, and Scollay Square here we come! With a drum and a horn we could do bur-les-cue and everything!"

"I'm not certain Mrs. Hodder would approve of burlesque—" I laughed at the picture that formed in my mind of Sherborn's finest swathed in feathers— and not much else. "But you're really right about the possibilities." I gave Ma a quick hug. "You see things that I miss. What would I ever do without you?"

"Aw, shucks." Ma blushed. "We just got us a good partnership going is all."

"Right." I pulled back from my wiry friend. Whatever *would* I do without her when I was released from Sherborn? I tried to shake the image from my mind: me on the free side of Sherborn's walls, Ma forever entombed within. I couldn't think about it now. Keep taking it one day at a time.

"Let's get started on fixing up the place for *our* show." I rubbed my hands with sufficient enthusiasm to banish my worries. "I'll bet there's enough junk here to make rocks and pirate ships and all sorts of props!"

I lunged toward the nearest pile, raring to go.

Ma hauled me back. "One little minute, Libby girl."

"What now?"

"We all got to learn a few things from past happenings—"

"What are you talking about?"

"Well, I ain't referrin' to how my dearly departed Harold got his just rewards. That were a necessary piece of past events."

"Then what were you referring to, Ma?"

She offered a meaningful look, furrowing the

lines on her leathery face. "The superintendent? Permission?"

"Oh. *Permission.*"

A knock on the door.

"Enter!"

A little half-curtsy.

Mrs. Hodder glanced up from the papers on her desk. "What is it, Libby?"

"Permission. I've come to ask permission, ma'am."

The superintendent squeezed out a small, satisfied smile. "Excellent. 'Those who cannot remember the past are condemned to repeat it.'"

"My memory is fine, Mrs. Hodder. No repeats are necessary."

"And Mrs. Wilkinson would have me shut down our solitary-confinement program? Not during *my* tenure. Not with such satisfactory results!"

I bit my tongue.

"Well, Libby, get on with your request. I'm a busy woman."

It took longer to put order into our new theater than anyone would have thought. I was still wiping streaks of grime from my face weeks later as Lena Colbrook stormed into the very heart of the chaos.

"What's happening, Doctor?"

"More news from Europe. The negotiations broke down. Austria-Hungary has declared war on Serbia. Russia is mobilizing more than a million troops near its western borders—"

I pointed at the stage rising before us, and raised my voice over the bangs and thuds and occasional curses as hammers slammed into fingers rather than nails. "And we've nearly got a stage!"

"Libby!" Dr. Colbrook was almost screaming. "There's a world out there!"

"Which none of us are going to be seeing for a good long time."

She shook her head. "You're an intelligent young woman. You can't just cut yourself off this way. War is coming, and our country might be neutral for a while, but sooner or later we'll be involved just as horribly as all the rest. America's efforts will go into wartime production. Everything unnecessary will be put on the back burner. That includes women's rights, women's votes—"

"In the meantime we've got the *Pirates of Penzance* to perform."

This time Lena Colbrook did scream. It was an odd sound coming from her staid, controlled body. It stopped all activity around us, too.

"Gilbert and Sullivan are not going to save the world!"

"Maybe not, Doctor, but they might set *us* free."

I turned to the stage and surveyed it with pride. We were all learning more than how to use our voices. We were learning how to work together. We were learning how to make decisions, to think for ourselves. None of that would have been possible without this production. Wasn't that a kind of freedom? "Make sure that flooring is rock solid, Rosie," I yelled. "It has to hold fifty-four people!"

"Aye-aye, Libby," she bellowed back.

I watched as Kid-Glove Rosie shoved a handful of nails in her mouth, spat one out, then gave it a satisfying smash with her hammer. The productive chaos resumed.

Although he wouldn't admit it, Sparky was getting too old to do heavy building work. But he'd done more than gardening in his life, and his carpentry skills became priceless to us after I made him chief of construction. It was Sparky who'd lined up my crew at the beginning of the new project to give them much needed lessons in sawing and hammering.

"Flo!" he'd bark. "You'll be handling that saw like a woman!"

Flo thrust out her ample breasts and leered. "In case you hadn't noticed, I *am* a woman, Sparky."

"Ay, well I won't be needing those kind of services."

"You're way past taking advantage of those kinds of services," Verity teased.

Sparky's sun-browned face changed to red. "In my day—"

"What about your day?"

"Never you mind," he huffed. "You got to put your whole body behind the motion. Here." He grabbed the saw from Flo and demonstrated. "That way. Now you be trying it."

Flo bit her lips and mastered her fleshy form. Her seesawing motion steadied. She broke through the two-by-four. "There! As good as any man!"

Sparky shook his head and moved on. "You'll be needing more power in that hammer swing, Molly. A redhead like you got to have more fire inside than's coming out in such wee little taps. Pound your nails in a rhythm. One . . . two . . . three," he banged the nail home with authority. "And she's in good and tight."

We all learned. And Sherborn's stage rose slowly from the floor into something impressive. Something imposing. Something solid.

Meanwhile, at the other end of the huge room, Mary and her kitchen helpers played hooky from their pots and pans as they worked on filling a backdrop with painted sky and waves. Sherborn's meals had become even more slapdash, but nobody noticed—or was willing to complain about—the changes.

The fifth of August, 1914, was a banner day for me. It was the day when I had my first costume fitting at last. Never had I so anticipated a new frock—not even when Quintus had carted me from the orphanage in my sackcloth straight to Filene's for a completely new wardrobe.

Agnes had a mouthful of pins and wielded them every bit as impressively as Rosie's mouthfuls of nails. I stood before her, glorying in the poking and prodding that I was certain would result in a masterpiece of high couture. Better than any of Quintus's overpriced French tailors. She tugged at the fine, almost sheer white lawn, then pushed me toward a full-length mirror she'd magically made appear in the wardrobe "salon" she'd devised at the rear of her domain.

"Whadda ya think, Libby?" Her words came from the pinless side of her mouth. "I got my hands on a nice piece of lace. As Mabel, it's yours. You want it tight up against your neck like a collar, sort of demure, or—" She grinned and almost swallowed the pins. I had to slap her on the back until she spit them all out.

"Or?" I asked.

"Or you want the neckline a little lower, a little more—"

"Interesting?"

"That's one way to put it."

My usual blue serge was flung over the nearest chair. That left only my undershift and drawers and heavy black lace-up shoes beneath the folds of soft white cotton. I experimented with the neckline, folding the cloth lower, and lower yet. "If I were to have a corset—"

"Corsets we got. All sorts were abandoned in that trunk room of yours." She pointed at a pile of yellowing underwear nearby. Just behind, Mildred looked up from the gold braid she was stitching on the Major-General's three-cornered hat.

"The laundry'll be glad to bleach one of them corsets for you. Go for the works, Libby. Give them very important people a thrill."

I was torn. "But I don't want to appear—"

"Wanton?" cackled one of the Swindling Twins.

"Like one of our favorite ladies of the street?" added the other.

"Here." Agnes unwound me from the cloth. "Pick yourself a proper corset and get into it. *Then* we'll decide."

I selected a likely garment and modestly ducked behind the mirror. I reappeared to allow Agnes to tighten the stays, then began all over again. More pins, more form fitting. Mildred tossed over a bright crimson strip of satin and it was wrapped around my waist. I held my breath and turned to the mirror once more.

"*Gad.*"

"Yes!" The entire machine room was avidly watching.

"Give 'em what you got, Libby!"

"Knock their spots off!"

I caught Agnes's eye in the mirror. "I don't suppose

that piece of lace could be worked around the bodice?"

"Agnes Cordoni can produce any frock on earth, in any style! In my day—"

"It's still your day, Agnes," I smiled.

"Well, it might be," she allowed. "If I had a few more tools to work with, like some decent adjustable dress forms, and—"

"When you get out you ought to set up your own shop. *I'll* come. And I'll send all my friends." I knew they were nonexistent, but said it to give her courage. "You'll be the toast of Boston's dressmakers."

"If the booze don't get me again."

"Why should it?" I preened a little more. "With such talent—" A new reflection in the mirror stopped me. Beyond my shoulder Lena Colbrook was striding down the long aisle between sewing machines. She was wearing her woman-with-a-mission expression, and waving a newspaper.

"Have you heard? No, I don't imagine you have. Superintendent Hodder just gave me the paper."

"I thought you had infirmary duty," I said.

Dr. Colbrook closed in on us. "The epidemic of smashed thumbs is long past." She halted and circled to wave the sheets of the *Boston Globe* at all the faces raised in anticipation above their machines. The *whirr* of busy needles and treadling stopped. "I thought you'd like to know—ought to know."

I suddenly felt naked with my breasts partially bared. I folded my arms over them. "Know what, Doctor?"

"Germany has declared war on Russia. The first shots have been fired." She continued her recital relentlessly. "Russia has invaded Germany. Germany is pushing into France, Luxembourg, and Switzerland. Not to mention invading Russia in turn. The first naval battle has taken place in the Baltic." She crumpled the paper. "That's not all. Germany also invaded Belgium, causing England to declare war on Germany—"

"Three thousand miles, Doctor Colbrook," I reminded her. "We've got the entire Atlantic Ocean between us. Not to mention the walls of Sherborn Prison."

The doctor studied me in my fine costume. "Fripperies. You've nothing on your mind but fripperies. All of you. I don't know why I even try to educate you." She spun and stalked out.

I dropped my arms to my side. Another glance in the mirror showed me the doctor was correct. Men were going to be shooting at each other. People were going to die. And here I was, fussing over the cut of my décolletage. The joy went out of my costume, out of me.

"Party pooper," Mildred muttered. "Always trying to change us."

"More like an—" Fanny Snodgrass began.

"*Anarchist!*" Freda Snodgrass finished for her twin. "First *reading.* Next thing you know, she'll be teaching us how to make bombs here in Sherborn."

I slowly unwound the sash. "No, that's unfair. Dr. Colbrook is a good woman. An intelligent woman. She just wants to make *us* as good as we can be, too. She wants to make us *think.* Why, oh why, can't such people have a sense of humor?"

My complaint was interrupted by another visitor.

"Libby Dodge?" the voice echoed through the entire length of the room.

It was Gladys, the once-again trustee.

I swallowed hard. Where Gladys came, trouble followed.

"Yes?"

"Superintendent Hodder wishes to see you. Immediately."

I ducked behind the mirror to claw out of my corset and slip the tired blue serge back over my head.

CHAPTER 14

I hadn't anticipated making another journey up the long flights of stairs to Superintendent Hodder's tower aerie quite so soon. The closer I got to the top, the more my legs slowed. A too-familiar ache returned to my stomach. The before-another-job ache. Being summoned by the superintendent was nearly as bad. What had I done this time? What rule had I broken? I halted at the final landing before her door.

I was *not* going back to solitary confinement. I'd be willing to attempt *anything* rather than return to solitary confinement. Poor Ruby still had days when she'd turn from perfectly sane to half mad. I now knew why. Purgative though my stay had been, once was enough. I didn't need to revisit my demons again. It took a human being of the strongest possible constitution and will to survive repeated stays in those dungeons. Maybe Ma McCreary could handle it.

After those last black days, I wasn't convinced I could.

I stood tall and raised my hand to the door. I'd go over the wall. Escape. *Anything.* My fist moved forward for the fatal knock—

The door came out to meet me, followed by Gladys the trustee.

"About time, Libby," the weasel whispered. "Where have you been?"

"None of your business. Not a single part of my life is any part of your business, Gladys." I pushed past her. "I believe the superintendent is waiting for me."

She was.

"Kindly close the door behind you."

I turned and shoved it tight, almost catching Gladys's nose in it. A pity. That would have cheered me enormously.

"Sit down, Libby."

I whipped around. "Excuse me?"

Mrs. Hodder pointed at a waiting chair. "Sit, please. We have something of importance to discuss."

I sat. I neatly drew my ankles together the way a well-bred young woman ought. Then I placed my hands demurely on my lap. It was necessary to try to calm the shakes working up my legs from those ankles to my knees and beyond. I opened my mouth.

Mrs. Hodder raised a warning hand. "I believe I'll be doing much of the talking, young lady."

I nodded dumbly and waited. Mrs. Hodder took her own good time sizing me up. Finally she began.

"It would appear that new evidence has come to light on your life before your incarceration here in Sherborn, Libby Dodge."

I let forth an involuntary squawk, then covered my mouth as if I'd sneezed. *What?* They'd discovered other jobs I'd done? *All* the jobs? Beginning with my training at Filene's? That had certainly never been my intention. All I'd wanted to do was *stop*. Escape from Quintus. I'd be in Sherborn forever. As long as Ma!

Mrs. Hodder squinted at some legal-looking papers set before her and carried on. "It seems that your guardian, a certain Dr. Quintus Wylie Gill?"

I slumped in defeat.

"It seems that this so-called guardian was in fact the instigator of your crime. A sort of depraved Svengali."

My spine straightened. Was there hope? I couldn't

keep my mouth shut any longer. "He's been exposed?"

"After removing several other young girls from a Boston orphanage and apparently—through the use of vile threats—training them in *thievery.*"

My mind reeled at the thought of Quintus Wylie Gill *exposed*. I smiled a beatific smile. A smile worthy of Mrs. Wilkinson. "Quintus has been caught? Please tell me he's really been caught! Please tell me he's been put on trial, and sent to the nastiest prison possible—"

Shockingly, Mrs. Hodder smiled back. "All that seems to have been accomplished."

I leaned back in my chair, kicked out my legs and continued to beam. Quintus was behind bars. He wouldn't be hovering outside the walls of Sherborn to snatch me back into his life when I was released. His career as a well-bred Fagin was over. I stopped beaming. "For how long? How long will he be imprisoned?"

"Oh, a good ten-year minimum, my dear. More if he doesn't relate well to the life. The state of Massachusetts frowns upon the corruption of minors."

"And the sanitarium?" I asked. "What's to become of his sanitarium?" And my poor mother.

"Apparently the state of Massachusetts is also taking that under its wing."

I offered a silent prayer of thanks as the superintendent shuffled the legal papers with complete detachment and glanced up. "Which brings us back to *you*."

"Me?" I had no idea what to expect next.

"You *have* adapted well to the life here, Libby." She paused. "Aside from that one minor lapse a short while ago. But I've taken the liberty of deleting your stay in solitary confinement from your official files."

"You have?"

"Yes, my dear. You seem to have become the heart and soul of our little community since Mrs. Wilkinson had the perspicacity to begin her choir—"

"And train us to perform Gilbert and Sullivan," I quickly added.

"Indeed. Odd how an opera could have such effects."

I studied the woman. Had she really banished all memory of her former life of music so completely? How could anyone forget the effects of music once the discovery had been made?

She cleared her throat. "However, that leaves us with a small dilemma."

"A dilemma?" I parroted. Where was this conversation leading?

"Yes, a dilemma. Since you performed the robbery for which you were convicted under coercion . . ." She squinted at the fine print again. "And since—according to information which came to light in the course of Dr. Gill's trial—you were literally kept in a state of imprisonment in his sanitarium for several years prior to that event—"

"Yes?" I breathed.

"Well, because of all that, your conviction has been overturned." Mrs. Hodder gathered the papers together and tapped them into a precise pile.

"Which means what, ma'am?"

"Which means that you, Libby Dodge, have been unjustly imprisoned. Neither I nor the state of Massachusetts can return to you the time you have already served." She stopped. "We can, however, expunge your record of imprisonment."

"You mean I won't be an ex-convict for the rest of my life?"

"I've already said this. You will walk out of

Sherborn's gates a free woman, your reputation totally reinstated to you."

"When?" I asked.

"Immediately. Today, if you wish."

"Today?" I gulped. "But Gilbert and Sullivan! The *Pirates of Penzance*! I'm Mabel, one of the leads!"

"I'm certain Mrs. Wilkinson will be able to train a replacement."

I fumbled up from my seat. "But I've got the voice! I've got the trills! I've got a lovely costume! What will Mrs. Wilkinson think if I leave her in the lurch? What will Ma think, and Sal and Rosie—"

Mrs. Hodder stared at me. "I'm certain they'd think you were acting within your full rights."

I took a deep breath, trying to calm myself. I had to get some perspective. Yet I knew there was only one way to respond to this unexpected boon. "Acting within my full rights is not the same as acting with my full heart."

I couldn't let them down. I'd be letting down all of Sherborn. I faced the superintendent.

"Is it possible, Mrs. Hodder . . . Is it possible I might be allowed to stay until we finish the production? Until we actually give our performance?"

Another long stare from the superintendent. "Mrs. Wilkinson has been saying all along that you were a remarkable young lady. I'll have to pay more attention to our chaplain's intuition in future." She smiled more freely. "Yes, I suppose Massachusetts can afford to pay for your room and board another few weeks."

I breathed naturally again. "Thank you, Mrs. Hodder. Am I excused now? I have to check progress on the stage, and the sets—"

"You're excused."

I made to turn, then faced her again. "One last thing, if you please. I'd rather no one was aware of this, this *situation*. Nothing should interfere with our coming production."

"I'll try to honor your wishes, within reason."

"Thank you."

I darted from her office, then skipped down the stairs.

Free. *Nearly* free at last. Free of prison, but even better, free of Quintus Wylie Gill.

At rehearsal that afternoon, Ma belted out her proud call to arms:

"Oh, better far to live and die
Under the brave black flag I fly,
Than play a sanctimonious part
With a pirate head and a pirate heart.
Away to the cheating world go you,
Where pirates all are well-to-do;
But I'll be true to the song I sing,
And live and die a Pirate King."

Tears streamed down my face unheeded. The lyrics were so *true*. And so *Ma*. I'd be leaving for that cheating world sooner than ever I expected. I'd be leaving Sherborn, where I'd been happier than I'd been since the age of seven. I dwelt on that thought a moment. It was an odd thought, yet a perfectly *true* one. I held on to it.

When Ma continued with her rousing "For I am a Pirate King!" I found myself shouting out in defiance with the entire chorus:

"You are!
Hurrah for our Pirate King!"

I finally found the presence of mind to haul out a handkerchief and swab my face as Ma rose to the climax of her performance:

> *"And it is, it is a glorious thing*
> *To be a Pirate King."*

I had to leave the assembly room before the dialogue began between Ruth and Frederic. The tears didn't want to stop. I wasn't fighting them anymore, though. Let them come. Maybe it's part of being free again. Free, even here in Sherborn.

Then I caught myself out in that corridor beyond the assembly room and forced the sobs to stop. If I wanted my little secret to remain so, I couldn't go all maudlin this way. I honked hugely into the handkerchief as Big Bertha shouldered her way into the hallway next to me.

"Back inside, Your Highness," she grunted.

"I just need a moment to compose myself—"

"Any composin'll be done with the rest of 'em." She glowered hugely, slamming a fist into her palm. "Two hundred females, most of 'em with their time of the month all at once. The curse ain't gonna rule this prison if I have any say about it. Inside."

"It's got nothing to do with—" my retort halted with the glare in the matron's eye. What was the point? I stiffened my shoulders, stuffed the damp hanky in my apron pocket and returned to the rehearsal. Now *there* was someone I'd never miss when I left Sherborn.

CHAPTER 15

The stage was built. Its varnish was dry and gleaming. To its rear—upstage according to theater lingo—the set department's backdrop of yards and yards of stitched and painted white duck was a dream of blue skies and dashing waves. The prow of a cutout ship jutted jauntily over stage right, flying a wonderfully ferocious black flag: the Jolly Roger with its grinning skull and crossed bones. Papier-mâché rocks and boulders littered the entire downstage area. Everything was in readiness. It was time to block out the show.

"Pay attention, ladies."

Mrs. Wilkinson had her baton of generalship in hand, but didn't really need it. We were all waiting for the next step.

"This is where our whole production comes together at last!" She slowly turned to take in the entire choir, scattered ever so reverently over that gleaming floor, and then the set. "Just like our very own Pirate King, it is going to be glorious!"

Ma beamed and hunkered down to listen. "We're game, Boss. Let 'er rip!"

"Thank you, Mrs. McCreary. Now, then, *blocking*." Mrs. Wilkinson set in to her explanations with vigor.

"Blocking is the act of showing the performers where to stand, so they don't bumble into each other by accident. It also involves the specific gestures you are to perform at that particular place and moment. All the *business* of your role. Your lines—which you all know—are your cues. They will tell you when to move in certain directions, or even when to vacate the stage. Am I making myself clear so far?"

Nods from everyone.

"Good. Now then, to make things a little easier"— she pulled a roll of sticky tape from her pocket—"I'm going make a few marks on the stage floor—"

A general groan rose.

"*What?*" Mrs. Wilkinson froze. "What's the matter?"

"I just buffed that floor!" Verity growled. "See the shine?"

"You're going to mess up our masterpiece!" Rosie

was outraged, too, as well she might be. She'd pounded in most of the nails.

"Oh dear." The chaplain stood there, for once unsure what to say next. It was Ma who came to the rescue.

"Listen here, all of you," she piped up. "I been to a lot of thee-ay-ters in my day, and never once did I see a gleaming stage floor. What I saw was paint and ground-in dirt. Scuff marks all over the place. Stains from tossed tomatoes and beer. Seems to me—" Ma nodded with expert decision. "Seems like the best kind of a stage floor is a *used* one. Gives it a little history, like."

I watched Ma's thought percolate through the crowd. I was proud of her again. She had so much basic common sense. She'd really only made one big mistake in her entire life. No, make that two: she'd had to marry Harold McCreary before deciding the relationship could only come to a fatal end.

Rosie made a move first. She picked up a foot and carefully scuffed her heavy shoes across the grain of her precious floorboards. Verity winced, then joined her. For solidarity I did a little jig atop the smoothness. In a moment the floor was vibrating with all the scuffling feet. This time Mrs. Wilkinson did bring down her baton.

"Enough! I do believe our stage has been initiated. May I start blocking now?"

She got grins for her answer and made a sweeping motion across the space, getting down to the real business at last. "Scene one. Pirates enter stage right. The Pirate King hangs on to the mast in the prow of the ship for his big number, while the pirates mill around below here."

Next she gestured to the rear of stage left. "The Major-General's daughters enter *there*"—she quartered the stage with her eyes, then bent to pat a neat little taped X in dead center—"and Major-General Stanley halts at *this* point to sing his introductions. After that . . ."

Blocking went along quite smoothly for a day or two. We all got used to the general comings and goings and the incidence of near-collisions almost ceased. At that point Mrs. Wilkinson began with the more subtle interactions between the leading players. This, alas, was nearly my downfall.

My part as Mabel really begins when I first set

eyes on Frederic, a young man whom all of Major-General Stanley's daughters agree is "a thing of beauty." He is, however, a *pirate*—which leads to certain moral quandaries. I was good with moral quandaries. In fact, you might say they were my specialty. Heaven knows I'd been dancing circles around my conscience for years under Quintus's thumb. So every time I staunchly stood up for Frederic in my big opening solo, Gilbert and Sullivan's words rang true for me—in more ways than one:

> *"Poor wandering one!*
> *Though thou hast surely strayed,*
> *Take heart of grace,*
> *Thy steps retrace,*
> *Poor wandering one!*
>
> *Poor wandering one!*
> *If such poor love as mine*
> *Can help thee find*
> *True peace of mind—*
> *Why, take it, it is thine!"*

Unfortunately, Frederic—really Verity—also

began taking my words to heart.

In the course of running back and forth like a dervish trying to accomplish my job as stage manager, I'd been ignoring Verity. I just figured that when the stage and set were all together at last there would be time enough to perfect the finer points in our duets on stage. A week before the scheduled performance, that time arrived. We met on stage, and what I saw made me gasp. It also should have given me a clue.

"What have you done to your hair, Verity?"

"What'd you think?" She strutted around, enjoying the bug-eyed response from the company.

Verity's light brown hair—formerly piled atop her head like the rest of us—had been cropped. Several *feet* of it were gone. What remained fell boyishly across her forehead and curled around her ears and neck.

"It . . . it looks wonderful!" It did, too.

Verity grinned. "My sacrifice for the show. To really get in character for Frederic."

Mrs. Wilkinson sagged against a papier-mâché boulder. "I'm not certain such a sacrifice was required—" She pulled herself together. "However, it *is* surprisingly becoming—"

"Looks cool and comfy, too." Ma eyed the latest

style with interest. "A body wastes a lot of time fussin' with all this useless hair—"

"One shorn cast-member will be sufficient, Mrs. McCreary." Mrs. Wilkinson's edict was definitive.

Ma sighed. "I hear you, Boss."

"Excellent. Now may we proceed? Frederic, Mabel. Front and center." She turned to the new Verity. "Frederic, as the chorus concludes with 'Take any heart—but ours!' you and Mabel exit stage right, arm in arm."

Verity nodded. "Yes, ma'am."

Mrs. Wilkinson tapped a finger against her cheek. "It seems to me, though, that before that moment, an embrace might be in order."

"You mean a little hug?" I asked.

"No. An *embrace*. Not as large an embrace as in the finale, of course, but an embrace nevertheless. With a kiss."

"A kiss? But . . . but—" I stammered.

"But what, Mabel?"

"But *Frederic* is really *Verity*, despite the haircut. . . ."

"Libby." Mrs. Wilkinson tended toward exasperation more and more the nearer we got to opening night. "This is *theater*. The art of make-believe."

I glanced at Verity. She was grinning again.

"Yes, Mrs. Wilkinson."

"Very well then, take it from the top, please, Dr. Colbrook."

Lena Colbrook launched the piano into my song. I warbled through the lyrics and my trills. I did love those trills! Each and every time I got so involved with them that I truly forgot about anything but the trills and Gilbert and Sullivan. I became Mabel.

Then the chorus concluded its piece. I came out of my trance. There was Frederic/Verity waiting with open arms. I rushed into them. We brushed lips. Exeunt.

Except that backstage, Verity still hung on.

"Verity—" I attempted to untangle myself. "You did that very believably, Verity."

"Thanks, Libby. But you can call me Frederic if it helps. For the onstage stuff, you know. And offstage, too . . ."

I backed off a step. "I'm not sure what you mean—"

Verity grabbed my arms. "Libby!" She gazed soulfully into my eyes. "Libby. I thought maybe you suspected, just a little. There wasn't much I could do, aside from sneaking you those flowers when you were so sick—"

"The wildflowers! They were lovely, and I do thank you for the thought, but—"

"Libby. I'm getting out soon. I've got a crib waiting for me. There's enough room for both of us. I'll keep it nice for you till you get out too. Then I'll take care of you! Protect you! You need protecting, Libby— from someone who cares."

She slowed for a deep breath, then added her clincher.

"My pimp sets a hand on you he's a goner! Please, Libby—"

Gad. It *was* possible to take Gilbert and Sullivan too seriously.

"Verity." I removed her hands as gently as I could. "Dear Verity. I've never had a nicer offer. Really and truly. Thank you. Thank you for cutting your hair, too—"

"I lied about doing it for the play. I did it for you. So you could see the real me."

I looked at the real Verity. "I like the real you, but you see, well—"

I didn't want to hurt her. I cast my eyes away from her lovesick ones and made another stab at ing myself from the delicate situation.

"Neither of us has had the opportunity to make the acquaintance of a really fine man, Verity," I began. "An honest, upstanding man." My voice took strength from my vision: a cross between Edmond Dantès and Cyrano de Bergerac, perhaps; with just a touch of *A Tale of Two Cities'* Sydney Carton. He loomed before me: a good man, craggy and strong— yet a man vulnerable to the right young woman. The image gave me hope. I faced Verity again.

"Even though my past experience with men has been . . . disappointing . . . I believe—I want to believe. Oh, Verity, I *need* to believe that such a man exists out there in the real world. Waiting for me." I paused to gather my final thought, then went for it.

"I think I have to give that man a chance, Verity."

This time Verity backed away. She rubbed at an eye. "You're a decent one, Libby. Through and through. You deserve your dream." She stopped and waited.

"Yes?"

"Can we still. . . will you still . . . do Mrs. Wilkinson's stage business with me?"

I smiled. "That's *theater*, like Mrs. Wilkinson says. A

good actress performs her role to the best of her ability. Always."

"Thank you, Libby."

Verity trudged off, but I stood there a long minute behind the side curtains of the wings waiting for my heartbeat to slow to something like normal. I needed Ma. I needed my geranium and the quiet of my cell. I laughed out loud. What I really needed was to get out of Sherborn for good and final. I needed to get back into that real world outside and find out exactly how ridiculous my dreams were.

CHAPTER 16

Reality kept getting more and more mixed up with make-believe in Sherborn.

In the middle of the afternoon only three days before our opening night, Mary the cook dragged me off with her set department crew to a stand of trees beyond the potato and turnip fields; even beyond the long rows of ripening corn. In the middle of the woods, she stopped.

"There!" She pointed.

"Where?"

"That row of wee birch. Ethel, my cook's helper? She was out here early hunting mushrooms for Mrs. Hodder's luncheon omelette when she spied 'em. Back she ran, scattering her whole basket of mushrooms to the winds, she was that excited."

I stared at the four very young, very thin birch sprouts. The skins of their trunks were a lovely mottled white and were delicately peeling, something birch trees did so well. Their leaves were dainty and green. "They're really great trees, Mary, but—"

"Don't you see, Libby?" She pounced on the nearest in line and gave it a great shake. "They're perfect! We can dig 'em up. Pot 'em."

"And?" I asked.

"It'll be the final touch to our stage design. Standing ever so graceful-like against them waves and skies of the backdrop. It'll all come perfect. Like a soufflé."

I laughed. Mary had surely never made a soufflé in her life—no less a perfect one. Spindly trees flopping all over the *Pirates of Penzance* danced through my brain. Still—

"Get some pots and shovels from Sparky, Mary. Ethel?" I turned toward the hollow-cheeked woman jiggling nervously nearby. "This is a much better discovery than mushrooms! You've figured out how to make our set really come alive! Thank you."

Ethel clasped her hands to her flat chest. Color spread over her face. "Oh, Libby. I did so want to do something special. Something that was *my* contribution."

My heart eased right out to Ethel. Here was

another woman whose life had been spent slipping through the cracks. How many of them were in Sherborn? How many floating in the outside world? Too many. I'd be joining them soon myself. And I hadn't yet determined how to keep myself from falling back into those cracks. There weren't nearly enough Mrs. Wilkinsons to save all those souls through music—or Lena Colbrooks to save their bodies and minds through education.

I gave her a little hug. "You've made your contribution, Ethel. Wonderfully." I shifted toward the others. "Do you think we can have them onstage tonight for our first dress rehearsal? That will give the players time to reblock their moves around the trees."

Most of the kitchen crew sprinted off toward the fields and Sparky's shed. I bent to reach for a mushroom.

"No!" Ethel knocked it from my fingers. "That one's poisonous, Libby. You just steer clear of mushrooms till after opening night! Steer clear of anything dangerous. You've got to protect your voice. The set department's counting on you!"

My fingers tingled for a moment. "Thanks, Ethel. I'll try to do that."

* * *

The first dress rehearsal arrived at last. All of Sherborn was in a total uproar again. Drab serge was scattered over the theater's auditorium as the chorus and players proudly donned their bright costumes. Agnes and her costume department crew stood close by, needles in hand to make the final stitch needed here or forgotten there. Then we were lined up around the steps to the stage, waiting to make our first entrances. Lena Colbrook launched into the overture.

"Just a minute, Dr. Colbrook," I called.

The music halted.

I took a deep breath and mounted the steps to center stage. This was the moment I'd been secretly planning and organizing. Why did it scare me to face my friends alone from this position? I reached for another deep breath, smiled, and launched into my piece. "Mrs. Wilkinson? Would you grace the boards with your presence, please?"

Mrs. Wilkinson made her entrance across the scuffed boards from the wings. "Whatever is it, Libby? I wanted to time our rehearsal tonight—"

Standing under the glare of what seemed to be every

electric lightbulb in Sherborn—liberated and strung across the stage ceiling by Sal and Rosie and their cohorts—I almost forgot my purpose and my lines.

"*Psst!* Libby! Chaplain . . . director."

Ma reminded me. And Agnes helped by thrusting a box over the apron into my arms. Everyone was waiting. A few giggles of anticipation were beginning to escape. "Mrs. Wilkinson?" I turned to her.

"Libby?" She looked bewildered.

"Mrs. Wilkinson." My carefully wrought lines suddenly flowed. "You are our chaplain. You are our music director. You adapted Gilbert and Sullivan for a production of their *Pirates of Penzance* they themselves would have cherished. But you are so much more. You've become our *friend*. In recognition of all of this, we got together—each and every one of us Sherborn women onstage and off—to give you this little token of our esteem."

I held out my arms and watched Mrs. Wilkinson's mouth work soundlessly. She accepted the box.

It was my turn to give the orders. "Open it."

Facing the audience, she obeyed. Mrs. Wilkinson attacked the long box with fumbling fingers. The flaps spread wide, and out came—

A pile of shiny satin.

"Unfold 'er, Boss," Ma yelled. "It's top of the line!"

"Reversible, too," Agnes pointed out. "Mauve or black. The latest fashion!"

Mrs. Wilkinson shook the cloth open. "An opera cape!" she gasped.

"For opening night!" the crowd roared.

"Thank you!" She dabbed an edge of its hem against one tearing eye. "Oh, thank you all so very much, my friends!"

Mrs. Wilkinson and I shared a hug, then she draped the cape dramatically over her shoulders and regally addressed Dr. Colbrook.

"The orchestra may now commence with the overture."

That wasn't the end to the lovefest for the evening. I was tidying up backstage after the rehearsal when Mrs. Wilkinson appeared with another box.

"What's this?" I asked.

"Something I've been saving for you, Libby. I never expected to be upstaged by you and the others earlier this evening."

"You do like your cloak? We sent off for the latest

patterns, and yards of fresh satin, not bits and pieces like with the costumes—"

"I *love* my opera cloak, Libby. I've never had a nicer gift." She thrust the box at me. Now it's your turn. Open it."

Confused, I attacked the box with my own fingers fumbling. And out of this one came—

"Oh! A *parasol!*"

I grasped the slim black stick with its silk cord and golden tassel and ever so carefully spread the ribs. The parasol opened to three tiers of bright white taffeta—sprinkled with rose-colored polka dots. It was the very same deep garnet rose as the final sash on my costume. The parasol was marvelously gaudy, marvelously gay. In short, perfect. I twirled it over my head.

"*Gad.* Now I'm going to have to relearn my blocking and choreography!" I turned to the chaplain. "Oh, thank you, Mrs. Wilkinson! But why?"

"Because you've become very special to me, too, Libby. My Jenny would have loved that parasol."

"And so do I!"

Our warm embrace was broken by one of Big Bertha's minions. "Lockdown. Now!"

* * *

I slept with my parasol that night. I truly did. I lovingly folded shut its ribs and tucked the taffeta next to me in bed so I could reach out and finger it every so often. Then I stared at the moon working its way past my window. It was growing with the summer's end. In two nights—Saturday night—it would be full. It would be absolutely and gloriously full in time to shine through those long (now brilliantly clean) windows in the auditorium and add its light to our Opening Night.

And then?

Sunday morning would arrive. I would be escorted to the gates of the Sherborn Prison for Women. I would be handed a ticket to Boston. Sparky would be waiting with one of the plow horses hitched to a wagon to drive me to the train station. That much I knew. But what else?

I twisted to stare at the moon. What else? What of clothes? What of money? What of a place to stay? There was no one out there waiting for me. *No one.* No home to return to. Not even Quintus's sanitarium. Even Filene's was closed on Sundays.

The moon had no answer for me.

I sighed over the impossibles I'd need to tackle to

physically survive in the reality beyond Sherborn's walls. More daunting still were the ideas waiting for me. As much as I'd tried to ignore Lena Colbrook's lectures, deep inside I knew I'd be returning to *her* world, too. It was a different world from that I'd encountered during my cloistered life with Quintus: one in which a woman's intelligence could be of more value than the clothes upon her back. So much for my nineteenth-century romantic fantasies. Brains, and votes, and the new war coming were likely to change the entire universe.

Oh Lord. I groaned, then reached for the parasol again. *Lord help me. This could be worse than solitary confinement.*

"Sal, could you possibly extricate yourself from the flies so we may begin?" Mrs. Wilkinson was consulting the pendant watch around her neck and tapping the toes of one well-shod foot. She was anxious to get Friday afternoon's rehearsal—our last dress rehearsal—underway.

"Soon as ever," Sal called down from the top of her wobbly ladder. "Just got to switch this last lightbulb for tomorrow night."

She jiggled her jury-rigged wiring, then pulled a fresh bulb from her apron pocket. Heaven only knew where this one had come from. There weren't many functioning lights remaining in the building. Beneath her, pirates and Major-General Stanley's daughters milled about. All of us watched her reach for the empty socket. All of us sighed with satisfaction as she carefully screwed in the bulb.

"All right, Molly," Sal yelled. "Let 'er rip with the juice!"

As one, the entire ensemble turned to the right stage wings where Molly Matches grasped the electricity lever.

"You want juice, you got juice." Molly pulled the lever.

Hisssssss.

Sparks flew. Second-Story Sal's new bulb exploded. Then it drifted down, down, down onto the apron of the stage, scattering more sparks as it went—onto all those papier-mâché rocks and boulders.

Those rocks were dry as tinder. Dryer. Ready to combust in bright puffs of flame. Next the fresh varnish would catch. I stood in a daze, imagining the inferno, seeing the end to everything. The end to all our months of hard work. The end to the *Pirates of Penzance.* The end to Gilbert and Sullivan.

"*Fire!*" Ma screeched.

Ma McCreary was made of sterner stuff than I ever would be. Leaping into action, she threw herself on the biggest boulder, rolling over and over with it, smothering the flames with her own body. Verity barely hesitated before diving for the next spark. Ruby and Rachel and Flo attacked the remainders. In a moment there was nothing but stamping feet, drifting smoke—and the sad charred remains of the set department's rocks.

"Ma!" I finally came to my senses and ran to her. She was curled in a ball, hugging herself. "Ma, are you all right?"

She coughed and scraps of burnt remains drifted from her arms and chest. Her voice came out deeper than usual. "Don't mess up your costume, Libby girl."

"Never mind the silly costume! Oh, Ma—" I gathered her in my arms. She winced. Then I noticed her hands. "You're burnt!"

Lena Colbrook pushed through the crowd. "Verity, Ruby, Rachel, and Flo. Report to the infirmary at once. I'll need to check you for damage. Mrs.

McCreary." She hovered over Ma and me. "Mrs. McCreary, that was a very courageous thing you did. I watched it all from the orchestra. You caught the brunt of the fire and shielded everyone else from it. Very courageous—and very foolish."

Ma hacked. "Weren't nothin'. I'd do a lot more for the show."

Dr. Colbrook shook her head in wonder. "Perhaps we don't need the idiocies of the outside world. Battles of valor can be won even here in Sherborn."

I stared her right in the eye. "Of course they can." Then I eased Ma up and we tottered off through the auditorium toward the infirmary. Behind us, Mary the cook clapped her hands.

"Pull yourselves together, set department. Praise be, it ain't noways worse than a few scorched pans. Clean up this mess! Then get off to the fields and lug some real boulders back here. The kind what don't get set on fire. We got a show to put on tomorrow!"

As Ma and I slipped through the door, Second-Story Sal's voice floated down from the flies. "*Damnation.* That's what comes of pilfering from the superintendent's office. You end up with a bad bulb."

CHAPTER 17

"**I**'m all right, I tell you!" Ma lay writhing on her infirmary bed, fit to be tied. "Get 'em to let me out, Libby girl—" She stopped for some heavy-duty hacking. "I gotta be Pirate King tomorrow night!" she wheezed.

"Calm down, Ma." I held both her arms steady while Lena Colbrook coated her fingers with cooling unguents, then began wrapping the burns. Behind us, Mrs. Wilkinson was wheeling over a little trolley filled with vapor-trailing porcelain inhalers.

"Sit up, Mrs. McCreary, and behave," the chaplain ordered. "If you truly want to be Pirate King tomorrow we're going to have to save your voice." She plunked one of the steaming containers on Ma's lap. "That means we'll have to clear the smoke from your lungs. *Inhale.*"

Ma inhaled . . . and heaved out a paroxysm of coughs. Lena Colbrook stopped constructing the mummylike wrappings on Ma's right hand to share a worried look with Mrs. Wilkinson. The doctor broke contact first and moved forward to the left hand.

"Hot steam every half hour all night," she prescribed.

Ma jerked away from the inhaler. "Now who's gonna be crazy enough to set me up with steam all night?"

"I am, Ma," I answered. "We all are. The *Pirates of Penzance* can't go on without its Pirate King."

Ma blinked. "Bless you, Libby girl. You're my four buried daughters all wrapped up into one."

"I love you, too, Ma." I shoved the steaming spout back into her mouth before things got too mawkish. *"Keep inhaling."*

It was a long night. Somewhere between half hours Ma's congestion eased up enough for her to nod off. I sat on the nearest bed to rest for a moment, and the next thing I knew sunshine was streaming across my face.

"What's happening? What—" I bolted up with a start.

"Relax, Libby." Mrs. Wilkinson was sitting next

to me, smoothing me back down onto the pillows.

Everything came back. The dress rehearsal. The fire. Ma. I forced my way up again. "Ma! How is she?"

Mrs. Wilkinson pointed. "Snoring blissfully." She shook her head. "Sometimes I almost wish I could be Belle McCreary."

"Without Harold," I inserted.

"Definitely without Harold," the chaplain replied. She cracked a smile. "And what about you, Libby? Do you think you've had enough rest for our big day?"

In answer, I swung my legs past her, reaching for the floor. "Oh, no!"

"What now, dear?"

"I'm still wearing my costume! Mabel's dress! And it's ruined!"

Perfectly on cue, a head poked through the door. "You up yet, Libby?" It was Agnes Cordoni. She marched in and tossed a Sherborn uniform at me. "Good. Get yourself out of that costume. The laundry girls are waiting to deal with it. And my team will take care of rebuilding Ma's pirate duds."

Agnes proceeded to collect both costumes with brisk efficiency, then was out the door, arms piled high.

I sat there in my undershift and drawers. "It's really going to happen, isn't it, Mrs. Wilkinson?"

"Yes, Libby. We've too much invested. Every last one of us here at Sherborn has too much invested. The *Pirates of Penzance* will go on."

Two hours before the show I was rooted before the stage in fascination. The set department's rocks were extraordinary. They were so big, so *real*. How on earth had Mary's scrawny kitchen helpers lugged so many of them all the way through the fields to this point? Not to mention levering them onto the apron of the stage . . . With the real boulders, and the real trees waving ever so slightly with the summer breeze flowing through open windows—all against the backdrop of sky and waves—the stage had the look and feel of a rocky Cornish coast at last. It was all so perfect. And disaster had made it so.

I couldn't pull myself away until the laundry girls arrived, my costume in hand.

"Here you go, Libby. Good as ever."

I reached out for the soft, summery cloth. Suddenly, along with the stage, everything else came into place. I was going to be Mabel. I *was* Mabel. I stretched my arms to magnanimously hug both laundresses.

"Don't Libby! You'll get the frock all creased again!"

Then I was laughing, probably with a touch of hysteria. It took Gladys to set me straight.

"Get a grip, Libby." She appeared from nowhere to pound me on the back. "We've still got the seats to set up. And Mrs. Hodder's guests are already beginning to arrive for sherry."

I gulped deep breaths and straightened the gown thrown over one arm. "Thanks, Gladys, I needed that."

"My pleasure entirely."

We stood edgily facing each other. Then I remembered I didn't need a case of hives just before the big night. I stepped back. Gladys tossed her golden locks, the glory of which would be hidden this evening under Major-General Stanley's tricornered hat.

"Libby—"

I never knew what Gladys might have said. An apology for her treatment of me? An apology for her life? Best wishes for the performance? A great clanking and clattering ended the moment.

"Everybody clear out!" Molly Matches roared from the rear of the auditorium. "We got chairs coming through!"

Lena Colbrook played the overture with finesse. I watched from the wings as the pirates trooped off their ship, singing the opening chorus with joyful vigor and British accents intact:

> "Pour, O pour the pirate sherry;
> Fill, O fill the pirate glass;
> And to make us more than merry
> Let the pirate bumper pass."

Ma remained at the mast, grasping with her burnt hands as if she couldn't feel a stitch of pain. She was absolutely splendid in the blue-and-white-striped cape slung from her shoulders, a garish turban wound round her head, and a wooden dagger stuck through her belt. When she launched into her pirate anthem her coloratura was rich and deep, mellowed by all the smoke she'd swallowed. After the last "Hurrah for our Pirate King!" I half expected the Sherborn women in the rear to give Ma a standing ovation for valor, but they were saving themselves. They were, in fact, very literally and painfully sitting upon their hands. Mrs. Hodder had lined up all two hundred of us after lunch to give us our marching orders.

"Very important guests will be with us tonight, ladies. *Very* important guests. Need I tell you that your future—and the future of Sherborn—depends upon how these guests perceive us?" She offered her iciest stare. "I'm sure I don't. You will be on your best behavior throughout the performance. That is all."

Now I was examining these Very Important Guests through a slit in the side curtains. There were more than I had anticipated—at least fifty of them filling the front rows. Who were they? What did they know about Sherborn or prison life? Well, I for one would show them that woman prisoners, women *convicts* had something to offer. All my friends would, too. We'd prove that we were human beings, just like them. We'd prove that we were not discards, like old dish towels ready to be tossed out with the garbage.

"Libby! *Psst!* Libby!"

Ruth/Flo was almost finished with her plaintive attempts to hang on to Frederic:

"Master, master! do not leave me,

    Hear me, ere you go!

My love without reflecting,

Oh, do not be rejecting. . . .

My love unabating

Has been accumulating

Forty-seven year—forty-seven year!"

Ruby was pulling at my sleeve. "It's time for our entrance, Libby!"

My first trills went over wonderfully well, then Gladys was prancing to her spot center stage, riding a broomstick hobby horse that had been Mildred's inspiration.

    "I am the very model of a modern Major-General,

    I've information vegetable, animal, and mineral;

    I know the kings of England, and I quote the fights

        historical

    From Marathon to Waterloo, in order categorical—"

Gladys was brisk, clipped, sardonic as she worked

through Gilbert and Sullivan's scathing commentary of modern society disguised as humor. She was brilliant, and she brought down the house as our Sherborn women loosened up enough to free their hands for raucous applause. Then all the rest of us had to do was finish the first act.

Kid-Glove Rosie and her bumbling policemen stole act II. They'd devised a bit of silly business in which they hid, cowering, behind those scrawny birch sprouts while the pirates advanced for battle. The trees may have tottered, but they never fell. And Second-Story Sal only swore once when Rosie's cops gathered their courage at last and backed her up rearend first against the sharp edges of a rock.

I still had *tarantaras* ringing in my ears as I launched into my final reprise of "Poor Wandering Ones!" As I finished my last trill and fell into Frederic's embrace, tears were streaming down my face. I didn't give a fig. We'd been good. We'd been *wonderful*.

It was over.

CHAPTER 18

But not quite yet. I gracefully raised myself from my final curtsy to watch Mary and Agnes Cordoni marching up the center aisle toward the stage. They were followed by their crews, and each was carrying a bouquet of lovely flowers from Sherborn's gardens. Every single member of the cast and chorus was presented with a bouquet. And each and every one of us received a standing ovation from the audience as the presentation was made. Then Dr. Colbrook was called forward for her bouquet. Finally, it was Mrs. Wilkinson's turn.

She emerged from behind the curtains to stride across the stage in a pearl-gray evening gown trimmed with rows of crystal beads. The flowing chiffon taffeta did her justice, and the midnight-black opera cloak spread over her shoulders completed the effect wonderfully. All fifty-four of us made a little space of reverence around her as she held up her hands and faced the audience.

"Dear guests, thank you for joining us tonight. From the applause I heard and the hats I saw flung into the air, I believe I can agree with you that our performance of Gilbert and Sullivan's the *Pirates of Penzance* was a success—"

She had to wait until the renewed applause stopped.

"Our women here in Sherborn have been working on this performance for nearly five months. I'm proud of my women. I'm gratified by their success. Most of all, though, I hope *you*—our honored guests—take this experience for more than just an evening's entertainment." She stared long and hard through the stage lights into the silenced and attentive auditorium before continuing.

"I hope you've learned a little fact about life tonight. I hope you've learned that prisoners are not so different from the rest of us. Thank you."

She turned to us.

"And thank all of *you*. This has been the proudest day of my life."

What could we do after that? We hoisted Mrs. Wilkinson and paraded her around the stage. By the time we'd settled down, the very important guests had filed out. No one was left in the auditorium—save a single blockish figure emerging from the shadows.

"Fun's over. Back to your cells, all of you. Lockdown in fifteen minutes."

"Big Bertha."

Her name rose like a sigh. One by one the cast and chorus of the *Pirates of Penzance* dispersed.

"Just a moment, Libby." Mrs. Wilkinson touched my shoulder. "Not you."

I turned. "But lockdown—"

"You're not a prisoner anymore, Libby Dodge."

"You knew?"

"I know."

I shrugged. "What next, then?"

"Next is a little visit to Superintendent Hodder's office. Some of our Very Important Guests have requested the pleasure of meeting you."

There were half a dozen of them mingling with Mrs. Hodder in her office. Mrs. Wilkinson presented them to me in a flurry of names:

"Professor Jordan, Professor Marsh, Dr. Proczniak, and of course, Mrs. Lowell, one of the most beloved patrons of the New England Conservatory of Music . . ."

The names flew by, but I registered only that final piece of information: *the New England Conservatory of Music.* I found myself leaning on my polka-dot parasol for support. I studied it carefully. Why was it still in my hands? Why hadn't I left it on stage?

"Libby?"

I started. "Yes, Mrs. Wilkinson?"

"These distinguished people came to our performance tonight to hear *you.*"

"*Me?*" I whispered.

"Yes, *you,* Libby Dodge. They're old friends of mine—faculty members at the Conservatory—and they graciously acceded to my request to give you an audition."

"An audition?" I blathered. "When? Where? For what purpose?"

One of the gentlemen pushed closer. "Forgive me for interrupting, Perle, but perhaps I might cast further light on the situation for our young lady."

I stared into his face. It was a fine face, full of fifty years of living. It was also an intelligent face. "Sir, Professor—"

"Jordan." He reached for my hand. I readied myself for his grip. Instead, he bowed and brushed his lips across it. "Entirely my pleasure, Miss Dodge. What Mrs. Wilkinson is attempting to explain is that we came to hear what she told us was a very fine untutored lyric soprano. Alas," he smiled, and it crinkled the lines around his eyes. "Alas, we fell under the spell of the young lady behind that voice. Your audition is complete, Miss Dodge." He turned to gesture at the others. "While waiting for your appearance here in Mrs. Hodder's office, a decision was made."

I swallowed hard. "If you would be kind enough to explain that decision to me, Professor Jordan—"

His smile deepened. "Enough drama. There's been quite enough for the evening. Miss Dodge, we at the New England Conservatory of Music would like to offer you a full scholarship to live and study with us, beginning immediately with the newly commencing academic year—"

"Live?" I squeaked.

"I assure you we have fine, wholesome accommodations for our students—both male and female—"

A home.

"—while you pursue our four-year degree program.

Voice lessons, of course, and music theory, and the dash of languages and humanities necessary to train a fine singer for the concert stages of the world—"

Music. Music and a home. Maybe even friends.

"Yes." I gathered every ounce of poise within me to stand tall and proud—not Mabel, but Libby Dodge at last. "Oh, yes. I would be honored to accept your offer."

When Sparky drove the wagon to a halt before the gates of Sherborn Sunday morning, all two hundred women were lined up in the courtyard to see me off. It was a little warm for the waning summer day, but I wore the pale-blue wool I'd arrived in, my silk straw jauntily pinned atop my hair.

I took a deep, cleansing breath to chase off the butterflies in my stomach. It wasn't the old before-a-job ache. It was something entirely novel: the flutter of future possibilities mixed with the throb of regret. I studied the harsh buildings looming around me. All those turrets and towers, all that gray stone . . . It no longer had the power to color my life. No, it wasn't the fortress of Sherborn I'd be missing. It was its inmates. The flesh-and-blood women who'd helped to save me from that grayness—who'd brought me out of my own grayness into life. I turned to them.

Ma was front and center, of course, followed closely by Sal and Rosie—then a gaggle of Ruby and Emma and Molly and Rachel and Verity. I hugged everyone good and hard, then lingered with Ma.

"I had a chat with Mrs. Hodder this morning, Ma."

She was knuckling her eyes. "Get it over with, Libby girl. I can't stand too much of this."

"Because you're such a heroine, Ma—" I grinned at her. "And because you're priceless through and through, our superintendent has kindly agreed with me that you need a larger room."

Her fists dropped. "Don't you be playin' with me, Libby."

"I wouldn't do that, Ma. Ever. You've made the honor class!"

Ma slung her hands on her hips. "Well, and it's about time! Didn't do no kowtowing, neither!"

"You certainly didn't." I smiled. "And I'm coming back to visit you at Sherborn, Ma. I've got special permission. Every single Sunday afternoon."

"*Pshaw.* You'll have too much studyin' to do at that there posh school. And you'll be needin' time to do some courtin' with a fine, upstanding young man, too."

I grinned. "There's Saturday afternoons for that, Ma."

"Get on with it, Libby," Sparky groused. "Ol' Dobbin here ain't too spry anymore. You'll be missing your train!"

I gave Ma a final hug, then tore myself loose to face the chaplain. "Thank you," I tried. "So much. For everything—"

Mrs. Wilkinson ignored my waiting arms. Instead, she raised hers, baton in hand. On the upswing, the choir of the Sherborn Women's Prison launched into song:

"Hallelujah! Hallelujah! Hallelu-u-u-j-ah . . . !"

If "Reformation" ever comes to any, it must come under elevating influences, and conditions of self-respect, self-reliance, honor, love and trust: penalties, degradation, distrust, disgrace never yet reformed any human being, and the more Reformatory people come to understand and regard that fact the better it will be for their work.

—*Clara Barton,*
Superintendent of Sherborn Prison for Women,
1883—1884

AUTHOR'S NOTE

Gilbert and Sullivan Set Me Free is fiction based on fact. It was inspired by a feature article my daughter discovered in the *New York Times* of June 21, 1914. "Women 'Doing Time' Give *The Pirates of Penzance*"—complete with evocative photographs—describes the remarkable performance given by the inmates of Massachusetts's Sherborn Prison for Women. One glance and I was hooked. This was a story that had to be retold.

I plunged into research on the history of women's prisons. They were inaugurated in the United States in the 1870s as a protective measure for women inmates themselves—women who formerly had been tossed into prisons like Sing-Sing to be casually brutalized by male convicts and male staff. I followed the progress of female prison reformers into the beginning of the twentieth century when this novel takes place. I learned about rules and attitudes that surrounded the prisoners. I learned about the crimes for which they'd been incarcerated. All of this I've attempted to re-create.

Sherborn is real. Clara Barton served as one of its superintendents on the personal pleas of Governor Benjamin Butler of Massachusetts. Her nursing work on Civil War battlefields, creation of the first missing-persons bureau to locate soldiers lost in action, and organization of the American Red Cross won Governor Butler's admiration. Barton's residency was a short one, but the institution had other high moments in the late nineteenth century. The early feminist Lucy Stone lectured to the inmates. Louisa May Alcott, the famed author of *Little Women*—whose health was permanently broken by her stint as a nurse in one of Washington's Civil War hospitals—visited to read for the women. Then Sherborn fell into the hands of more traditionally authoritarian leadership.

Most of the characters are totally products of my imagination. Two, however, were as real as the prison. Mrs. Jessie D. Hodder did serve as the superintendent of Sherborn for twenty years, from 1911 until her death in 1931. Over that period of time she evolved from a strict disciplinarian into one of the leading advocates of prison reform for women, even having Sherborn's name changed from *Prison* to *Reformatory*. Sherborn still exists today within the Massachusetts Department of Correction. It's now called MCI-Framingham, and it is a medium-security correctional facility for female offenders. The old Gothic complex once referred to as "a grim, dark, Bastille-like structure" has been surrounded by more modern buildings—one of them named in honor of Mrs. Hodder.

I'd like to believe that my second genuine character, Mrs. Perle Wilkinson, had much to do with Superintendent Hodder's change of heart. Mrs. Wilkinson *was* Sherborn's chaplain in 1914. She *had been* the chorus mistress for a D'Oyly Carte troupe of Gilbert and Sullivan performers. Mrs. Wilkinson *did* direct Sherborn's performance of the *Pirates of Penzance*. Fact stops there. The rendering of these two women is entirely my own.

Libby Dodge is also my own invention, but her inspiration was a real Sherborn inmate who received her parole just before *Pirates of Penzance* was scheduled to be performed. Like Libby, she elected to remain imprisoned until after opening night. Libby's crime of shoplifting was also based on a true phenomenon that hit upscale department stores during this period.

In bringing these women and the prison environment of 1914 to life, I hope my story becomes more than just a fairy tale. *Reformation* and *redemption* are very Victorian words. *Respect* and *music* are ageless. The number of women incarcerated today is significantly higher than in 1914. A serious reconsideration of all four of these words might be useful for contemporary penologists.